Praise for
Spring Flowers, Spring Frost

A *New York Times* Notable Book
A *Los Angeles Times* Notable Book

"*Spring Flowers, Spring Frost* is murky and capricious at times, yet with flashes of compelling wit and the frenetic syncopation of life about to be sucked back down a black hole. . . . Kadare is closer here to Swift than to Kafka; he cuts sharp and all ways."
—Richard Eder, *New York Times Book Review*

"Fans of the fantastical, veterans of Borges and Kafka, may recognize the familiar combination of the mundane and the extraordinary. . . . With a breezy fluency, [Kadare] solves his mysteries with a political and mythical flair."
—*Los Angeles Times Book Review*

"Throughout the book, images of icebergs, the Titanic, and enchanted snakes recur, all of which may represent Albania and its various misguided governors. The result is like a dream—seemingly full of stirring meanings whose interpretations remain tantalizingly out of reach." **—*The New Yorker***

"[Kadare's] mixture of the realistic and the allegorical, the crushingly mundane and the eerily fantastic, is probably the best way to capture the inherent contradictions of present-day Albania. . . . The result is a heady brew of local traditions and universal themes." **—*Washington Post Book World***

"Impish, blackly comic . . . Underneath all this literary playfulness . . . lurks genuine insight into the duality of human nature and the often two-faced relations between men and women."
—*San Francisco Chronicle*

"Mind-bending . . . Compelling . . . One often has the sense of having wandered into alien terrain, a Balkan universe with undertones of Borges and Kafka. . . . Be prepared to have your sense of reality nudged a little out of kilter."
—*Seattle Times/Post Intelligencer*

"A great pleasure to read. As an exercise in what writers from the formerly communist countries are now attempting, it is exemplary. As another strange and seductive work from Albania, a mysterious country for most of us, it is both instructive and hauntingly familiar." —*Washington Times*

"A rich, symbolic questioning of humanity's capacity for creating a murderless society . . . The predicament of human community, which may be human nature, is enough to send any man cowering back to the womb. Philosophical fiction of great poetry and power." —*Booklist*, **starred review**

"Kadare artfully portrays how an individual is affected when his society is suddenly released from long oppression. Highly recommended." —*Library Journal*, **starred review**

"A folktale of enchantment and transformation . . . as spare and haunting as anything Kadare has ever written."
—*Kirkus Reviews*

"The juxtaposition of ideas and bizarre images is alternately beautiful, peculiar, and provocative, as Kadare once again provides an excellent glimpse at the difficult nature of life in a politically unstable land." —*Publishers Weekly*

"In Ismail Kadare's latest novel, Albania awakes from the isolation and terror it experienced under communist dictatorship. . . . Between the chapters that tell this story is a series of 'counterchapters' in which the writing breaks free from the restraints of naturalism and where Kadare shows his virtuosity as novelist and poet. . . . Each is handled with masterful skill."
—*Review of Contemporary Fiction*

Spring Flowers, Spring Frost

Spring flowers, Spring frost

a novel

Ismail Kadare

Translated from the French
of Jusuf Vrioni by David Bellos

Arcade Publishing • New York

FIRST NORTH AMERICAN EDITION

First published in France under the title *Froides fleurs d'avril* in 2000 by
Librairie Arthème Fayard

Original title in Albanian: *Lulet e fltohta të marsit*

This is a work of fiction. Names, places, characters, and incidents are either
the products of the author's imagination or are used fictitiously.

Library of Congress Cataloging-in-Publication Data
Kadare, Ismail.
      [Lulet e fltohta të marsit. English]
      Spring flowers, spring frost : a novel / Ismail Kadare ; translated from
      the French of Jusuf Vrioni by David Bellos.—1st North American ed.
      p. cm.
      ISBN 1-55970-635-X (hc)
      ISBN 1-55970-669-4 (pb)
      I. Bellos, David. II. Title.

      PG9621.K3 L8513 2002
      891'.9933—dc21   2002020877

Published in the United States by Arcade Publishing, Inc., New York
Distributed by Time Warner Book Group

Visit our Web site at www.arcadepub.com

10 9 8 7 6 5 4 3 2 1

Designed by API

EB

They were really flowers
But March was gone
Or else it was March
But the flowers were not real

SPRING FLOWERS, SPRING FROST

CHAPTER 1

AS HE WAS CROSSING THE INTERSECTION, Mark Gurabardhi
noticed a crowd of people, which was growing by the
minute, gathering on the right-hand side of the street. Most
likely he would have walked past without a second glance if
he hadn't heard someone say the word *snake!* — spoken not
in fright but in astonishment.

A snake at this time of year? Now that was out of the ordinary. . . . Mark went over to the knot of bystanders to see
what was going on. Most of the people standing around were
passersby, looking on just as he was. "Holy smoke, it really is
a snake!" someone said, as they all shuffled around to let new-
comers get a look. "But how can you tell if it's dead or alive?"
One glance was enough to tell Mark that it was neither dead
nor alive, but just hibernating, like a normal reptile.

Two youngsters (something about them made it clear that, without specifying how, they were the ones who had unearthed the snake) flashed their eyes in pride at the crowd. To demonstrate their rights of ownership, they poked the creature this way and that with a stick. When they lifted the reptile off the ground, people shrank back, but each time they did, someone in the crowd piped up with a "Don't worry, frozen snakes don't bite, and even if you do get bitten, it's not dangerous, the venom's too weak, like it's diluted by the cold. . . ."

A man in a felt hat seemed to be looking for a target for all his pent-up anger. "We've come to a pretty pass," he seemed to be saying. "Where but in Albania do you get minds as warped as that? No, we don't get up in the morning to do something useful, we get up with some crazy idea in our heads — unearthing sleeping snakes! What've you got between your ears, you little perverts? You wouldn't lift a finger to help save those antique vases or ancient bronzes people are forever digging up all over the place these days — oh, no, you wouldn't, but you don't miss a beat when it comes to finding horrors like this!"

Two others were discussing what to do with the snake. You could bury it again where it had been found and let it wait for warmer weather, as nature intended; or you could put it by a fireside — you'd have to be very careful, all the same — and let it thaw out.

"Have you all lost your minds?" another bystander blurted out. "All winter long we've all been frozen to the bone. Nobody cared a fig about us when we were cold — and now we're supposed to worry about some lizard?" Then an old woman chimed in. "Everything's gone to wrack and ruin, mark my words. I've been around for many a long year, God knows, but I've never seen anyone try to stop a snake from hibernating in peace!"

Mark turned around and was about to move on. His old friend Zef, if he'd been there, would surely have seen a symbolic link between this frozen reptile and the present state of affairs. Only two weeks ago, when they'd been chatting about the way things had gone in their bizarre world these past few years, Zef had likened the monstrosities of today's Albania to the ancient tale of the girl who had married a snake. And he'd added, with dark foreboding: All these *faces* that change their masks from one day to the next, like in some Greek drama . . . they don't inspire a lot of confidence.

Mark felt a pang of guilt for not having asked about his friend, whom he'd not seen since then at the office or in the café.

He looked up as a police car went by. The spirals of black dirt that it raised in its wake seemed angry at being dragged out of their slumber, but then slowly settled down before returning to rest on the somnolent highway.

Though the patrol car had been moving briskly along, Mark managed to get a good look at the policeman's face. Sitting in the front passenger seat, the officer had even seemed to turn slightly so as to look in Mark's direction.

He'd been tempted to yell after him: Mind your own business, big boy! He hated people turning around to look at him. In this instance, he disliked it even more than usual, since he'd realized that each time he ran into the officer in the café, the man looked at him with an ever more inquisitorial eye. Not all that long ago, of course, he thought with a sliver of a smile, he, like everyone else, would have been utterly distraught at the very idea that he might have inadvertently said something that could be taken two ways, even if it wasn't something actually forbidden. Nowadays, strangely, he would almost like to feel he was being watched, at least a little. . . . But it was late, far too late, for that, as for so many other things.

When a second vehicle — an ambulance, this time — went hurtling past in the same direction as the patrol car, Mark was convinced that something really unusual had happened.

As long as they're not rushing about like that on account of the snake! He dismissed the thought almost as soon as it had occurred to him.

As he arrived at the building where he had his studio, his mind wandered back to the strange story that Zef had told him: a girl engaged to a snake, then the wedding feast, the heartrending old tunes, the first night. . . . Whenever he remembered this part of the story, he could rarely refrain from taking a deep sigh.

Before he opened his front double door, his attention was caught by the right-hand leaf. It looked as if something had struck it quite hard. Then he remembered: it was the same dent he'd noticed a week before. He'd thought then that someone must have tried to break in.

The windows of his studio hadn't been cleaned for quite some time, but there was still plenty of light in the main room, maybe even more than needed. He turned toward the easel, with its unfinished nude, then cast his eyes at the other paintings he had hung willy-nilly here and there. There were some stacked on the floor, mostly facing the wall. Though they had been stored here for some time now, Mark knew by heart where to find every one of his unhung works: *The Delegate, The Festival of the Loaves, Highland Spring, Miner with Lamp. . . .*

He went back to his usual position at the easel, inspected his brushes to see which he would use, and lightly touched the unfinished painting between the legs, where he had barely begun to brush in the shading of the delta. I just hope she hasn't had the bright idea of shaving her pubic hair again, he said to himself as he glanced at his wristwatch. She should be here any minute. They'd recently had a slight argument about her pubic hair. He'd done his best to try and explain that it was not only a question of his own personal taste as a male, but it was above all a question of art: he simply could not put into his painting the kind of sanitized pubis that you see in porno movies or fashion parades. She had not been easy to persuade.

He checked the time once again. As always after they had been apart for a while, he was eager to spot little changes in her physical appearance. But as she was coming back from the capital on this occasion, he felt not just curiosity but the sharp pangs of a quite specific desire.

To get her off his mind, he puttered about the easel, put his brushes in order, looked at his paint tubes, pressed a couple with his fingers. For no particular reason, he wondered if he had been spied on these last few years. Many other people had also been asking that same question recently. It was said there had been quite a few stool pigeons, especially among writers and artists.

His eyes came to rest on the blotches of color on the canvas that stood on his easel. Venetian red. Van Gogh yellow. Prison blue. Ah, yes. That was the color that had got his old friend Gentian into the camp at Spaç.

He picked up a brush and started to mix colors on a blank corner of the canvas, the way he usually did to warm up, or when his nerves were on edge. He took two steps back to inspect the blotch. He'd once heard someone say — or had he read it in an old history book? unless he'd actually thought it up himself, under the influence of the conversation or the old book — that before the great fire of Voskopoja, intimation of disaster had appeared on painters' canvases. A disturbing shade of red that had never been seen before began cropping up here and there.

He almost smiled to himself. So what color would be the right one for the times they were going through? It was often called a "period of transition." In other words, hermaphroditic, or, in the old language of the people, "a bitch and a dog." He looked at the patch of color he'd mixed to divine the times, and curled his lip. It was a dull and murky gray. One of the two — Time, or he himself, who had created the shade to express it — was dead to the other. At least that's the way it seemed.

Then he heard his girlfriend coming up the stairs, almost running. She'd had her hair done in a new style, and it suited her; when he kissed her, he smelled a new perfume.

She poured forth news and gossip from the capital as she took off her clothes. There were more disturbances among the student population. What was more, the BBC had broadcast a speech by the pretender to the throne, apparently giving new hope to the monarchists, who had reestablished a political party.

Mark had the impression that her words became clearer and clearer as more clothes fell from her body. . . . There was a rumor that the state was going to be parceled out, shared by the people . . . in other words, all the assets of the nation, the fruit of forty-five years of socialism. . . .

He found a special thrill in watching her get undressed in this way, with both of them pretending not to know why she was stripping — to pose for the portrait, or to make love. It was a convenient ritual, especially on days when they were angry with each other. A minor quarrel could stop him from kissing her, could make her reject the merest caress of her hair, but taking off her clothes could be seen as having absolutely nothing to do with their squabble. Her gestures simply fulfilled her role as an artist's model, even if every movement she made to remove her clothes also increased Mark's desire.

There was a story circulating that the ministry of justice had legalized gay and lesbian associations, even if the names of the organizers were still being kept secret. A publishing house specializing in works by celebrities had just been founded.

"Well, well," he said as he looked under her armpits. "You've removed it all?"

"Yes," she replied, "but, as promised, I've not touched anything down below."

"Did you have any particular reason for the armpits?" he muttered.

"Same as everyone else," she said, articulating every word separately. "In Tirana, everybody does it."

She took off her panties, and Mark observed that her pubic mane was intact.

An Association of Young Idealists had also been established, she went on. And another group with a rather surprising name: the Post-Pessimist Association. The latest buzzword for insulting someone: "Megabugger!" As for the students from a certain university, they were allegedly planning another demonstration under the slogan "Down with the people!"

She laughed a pink laugh between each of her pieces of gossip; her cheeks were turning crimson, and her eyelashes seemed heavy enough to crush any tears beneath.

"So you don't want me to sit?" she teased, as he pulled her toward the bed.

"Afterward, my darling . . . It's Sunday," he added a moment later, "the offices downstairs are empty, so you can yell all you want."

She did indeed scream, in due course, but not as much or as loud as he had hoped.

"Don't you want to do any work today?" she asked afterward. Instead of going up to the easel, as he usually did once they had gotten up, he was standing in the bay window, in a dream.

He could imagine that his own eyes betrayed disappointment and frustration, just like the last time that something of this sort had happened between them. He presumed rather vaguely that such regret was like the loser's last consolation, when a love affair begins to cool off. Maybe his only hope of recovering the attraction he felt he had ceased to hold for her was to sacrifice his painting (at least, provisionally) by invoking a spiritual crisis, or the feeling of being misunderstood as an artist.

"So what's this business about sharing the state's assets?" he asked without turning around. "That strikes me as pretty strange."

She frowned before answering.

"To be honest, I didn't really understand it myself. . . . I think they mean that, as the state was socialist . . . in other words, the property of everyone . . . now that the system has changed . . . a share of it can go back to each and every person. . . . But I'm not really sure."

"I see . . . ," Mark mumbled.

The disturbing screech of a police siren could be heard outside, then a screaming motor. From behind the window, Mark watched the patrol cars rush past.

"That's the second time the police have come tearing past."

"Oh, I forgot to tell you: on my way over I ran into a girlfriend who said there'd been a holdup at the National Bank."

"A holdup at the National Bank?" Mark sounded as though he could not believe it. "Are you sure?"

"Oh, yes, quite sure."

"A heist, a bank robbery," he muttered, as if talking to himself. "Strange-sounding words . . . Our ears aren't used to them, are they?"

"Yes, that's what I felt when I heard the story, too."

She asked him for a cigarette, and as he brought his hand nearer to light it for her, he could see she was trying hard not to smile.

"Maybe it's a terrible thing to say," she said, "but when I heard that word, it seemed, like, how can I put it — it sounded really smart, like something from the West."

Mark burst out laughing.

"That's true enough! Our ears are accustomed to something quite different!"

He could have added, Such as "sheep rustling," "stealing a

rug," or even "damage to the socialist heritage," but all of a sudden the notion that her leaving him would be a catastrophe cut his train of thought off sharp, as with a kitchen knife.

For a while now, ever since he had gotten it into his head once and for all that everything having to do with her was facing forward, toward the future, and everything relating to himself was turned backward, toward the past, conversations of this sort frightened him.

He went back to the bed where she was still lying naked, and whispered into her ear:

"And if I gave up painting, would you still . . ."

He said "love me" so quietly that she only heard the last syllable, and even that was almost completely muffled.

She almost bit her lower lip. When she had come into this studio for the first time, three years ago, a shy girl though not a virgin, she didn't hide the fact that she had been attracted above all by Mark's fame as a painter. She realized in due course that he wasn't as well known as she had imagined, but she had remained no less attached to the man.

Mark did his best to mask his newfound fear of her leaving him, since he was convinced that if she noticed it, she really would dump him on the spot. For the time being, he felt she was the only gangplank he had toward the future, and that if the plank were to break, he too would collapse in a heap.

"I asked you a question," he said with his mouth close to her ear, as if he were concerned to have his message travel the shortest distance possible. Now he felt surprised at having dared broach a subject that terrified him above all else.

She kept her eyes lowered, and as Mark looked at her eyelids it struck him that, of all the parts of the human body, the tips of the eyelashes gave by far the most reliable reading of guilt.

"Yes, of course," she answered. "And even . . . maybe" (Good Lord! she too was skirting around the fatal word), "maybe even more than . . ."

In any other situation her answer would have troubled him. What was this "maybe" that referred to his art? Maybe it would be better if his art ceased to exist? Maybe it would be better if it were just a mistake, a source of misunderstanding, an obstacle between them?

At a different time, the same thought might perhaps have occurred to him, but he had in his mind's eye the still-sharp image of the disappointment he'd felt just a moment ago when she'd said, "Don't you want to do any work today?" So he persuaded himself that her vague answer to his question didn't warrant his doubting her right now.

He kept on stroking her between the legs, and she did so too, with an uncharacteristic lack of inhibition. And it was she who took the initiative, pulling him on top of her, so that Mark didn't have time to remind her once again that it was Sunday and that the offices downstairs were closed. She launched immediately into a deep-throated groan to which he was quite unaccustomed.

COUNTER-CHAPTER 1

STRANGE TO SAY, no one could remember what offense the girl's family or clan had committed. The terrible offense that could only be redeemed by her sacrifice.

When her father had summoned her to the guest room to speak of it, she bowed her head as she waited for the sentence. It is hard, he warned her a second time, but for the second time, she replied, "Whatever it is, I shall obey, Father." She had resolved to submit, whether it meant being shut up in a nunnery, marrying a ninety-year-old, or, worst of all, being walled up in the foundations of a new bridge.

She had made her decision. . . . Even so, when she heard the actual sentence, she went as white as a sheet. What did you say, Father? I am to marry a snake? The hope of having misheard evaporated on the spot. Yes, she was indeed committed to becoming the spouse of a snake. Not of a man so named because of his treachery, his looks, or for some other reason. She would be the wife of a real, an actual snake.

In mid-October the news of this monstrous union shook people more than the north wind. They were stunned. It's one thing to commit something so outlandish, they said, but why make it public? Others, who knew that publication of the strange marriage was a formal part of the agreement, kept their mouths shut.

The girl's house echoed day and night with knocks on the door. People had all sorts of reasons for dropping in: to commiserate, to turn the knife, or just to find out more about the case. . . . Some came with questions: So why did you accept? So why didn't you ask me about it first? And others with advice: Break your promise! . . . No, don't break it, because there is worse. . . . There are even more fearsome things. . . .

By stages, fewer and fewer people remained in a state of shock. When all is said and done, the whole business should be treated more calmly, people said. Of course, hearing about it was enough to raise the hairs on the back of your neck, but when you thought about it more carefully, it wasn't such a dramatic affair after all. What was called a marriage with a snake could be seen as something rather different. You could take it as a commitment to keep a snake in the house. An insane commitment, of course, but did that make it so special in this crazy world of ours? Keeping a snake in one's home was not especially unusual, in any case. The very saying, "I've nourished a snake in my bosom," proved that the custom had once been quite widespread in Albania. Not to mention countries like faraway China or India, where people bring up snakes in their homes like we raise chickens. No, no, the business should not be taken in such a tragic vein. A commitment of this kind was just a kind of punishment, or a mark similar to those that Jews and convicts used to be obliged to wear; in other words, a tax or tribute that had to be paid to redeem some serious offense. An offense that might otherwise have required the sacrifice of a human life . . .

What many people had called a sinister whim, or a frantic desire to crush the Other, or an example of Albanian lunacy, or a misshapen fantasy, or a compound of shame and horror, was in the end carried out. Like the publication of the engagement, the wedding ceremony was one of the necessary conditions. The marriage rites were thus celebrated in the normal manner, except that the church kept a clearly disdainful distance, and that instead of the bride going to the groom's house, the groom was brought to his bride.

The snake came in a wicker basket lashed to the back of a horse, with an escort of armed paranymphs led by their chief, as for a real wedding. Then the wedding verses were sung, shots were fired, and finally the paranymphs left as they came, on horseback. Night fell, and the newly wedded wife, known henceforth as "the snake's wife," was led to the nuptial chamber, where her spouse awaited her.

You can imagine what sort of a night the household spent. And the horrors were not those of the immediate family alone. No one in the whole village slept a wink. Everyone waited to hear a scream of misfortune or despair. The scream of the young wife bitten by her husband. Or else the wailing of the family as it discovered its daughter dead. Or a scream of God knows what in the face of such a monstrous error.

But the night passed without incident, and dawn when it came was just as calm. As they were sure that the new day would recompense their long wait, people allowed themselves to drop off for a bit in the small hours of the morning. To their considerable surprise they learned that curiosity, if it is allowed to go too far, tends to become painful.

The sun rose. Villagers flocked gingerly toward the house; then, abandoning their initial timidity, they knocked on the door. After all, they were from the same village, and had no reason to pretend they were unconcerned about what had gone on between those walls.

When the family showed them all in with a smile, the villagers were dumbfounded, and remained speechless when, before they had expected it, the young wife appeared, looking quite resplendent. Her face and hair were still made up for her wedding; as she moved about the house, she radiated contentment.

They could not take their eyes off her. Her face glowed gently, as if caught in the reflection of unseen mirrors, her lips formed just the beginning of a smile, and her eyes seemed bathed in dew. She was a resilient girl and had managed to hide her distress the whole summer long. Now it was not sadness but joy that she was failing to conceal.

She had obviously lost her wits. She had put up with that abomination as best she could, but in the end she had broken like a glass. Poor thing!

That was the first reaction that could be read in people's eyes. But then, with furrowed brows, they worked out a different explanation: the family must have killed the snake during the night. That was why they appeared to be free of anguish.

With that understanding in their heads, and expressing tacit approval with their eyes, the villagers left the house, feeling just as relieved as they imagined the family to be. So that was how it had turned out. Of course it was the only solution. They had thought of it often themselves but had never dared say it aloud for fear of committing a sin.

Toward the end of the afternoon the snake's masters reappeared in the village. They were out of breath, and had a menacing air about them.

"The husband!" they yelled from the doorstep. "We want to see the husband!"

The bride's father had been expecting this visit. He asked the men in, and took them up to the newlyweds' bedroom.

The serpent lay there peacefully, all coiled up, at the end

of the conjugal bed. The men went closer, inspected the reptile with all due care, then offered their apologies to the master of the house for having doubted him without reason. These days the world had become so evil and twisted. . . . Horrible suspicions had been whispered. . . .

"No matter, no matter," their host replied. "There's nothing surprising about that. Is not the world itself a doubting without end?"

As week followed week and month followed month, the villagers' curiosity fell off, like the yellowing leaves that fell to the ground and rotted away. The weather turned cold, the rains came, and fires were once again lit in the hearths. As they always did at the onset of winter, people kept themselves wrapped up indoors.

In the house that the snake had entered as a bridegroom, life went on as if everything was normal. The young wife grew more beautiful by the day. Not her eyes alone, but her whole body expressed joy. Her breasts, which had been small, grew larger, and her hips swung with a new vitality. All that remained was for her to say to her lord and master: Thank you, Father sir, for having got me a husband. Though she never put it in words, her looks expressed the thought unmistakably.

When evening came, she would stand at her mirror for a good long while arranging her hair, putting on her makeup, and then going up to the nuptial chamber. In the morning she would rise looking weary, but just as splendid as the day before.

So that's the way of this world, people used to say. One day you think everything is quite hopeless, and then all of a sudden you find a way to salvation.

So we should get used to snakes? others objected. Oh, no, no, no! She can carry on if she wants, but not us, never!

The womenfolk got even more excited when they realized that the young bride could even go to church or to a dance with her husband, like any other married woman.

But wait a minute, hold your horses, you women! the men would protest. Don't take things so dramatically! Haven't you ever seen a groom that turned out to be a hunchback? Or a bride who turns out to be blind when the veil is lifted? This one, at least, didn't hide the fact he was a snake! He was honest enough to show himself in the form that God gave him!

The story of the marriage with the reptile, which had begun in mid-October, seemed to come to an abrupt end on the night of the following January 17. That evening, as if she had foreseen that it would be her last night in the company of her snake-spouse, the young bride spent even longer than usual primping and arranging her hair. Then she lit the fire in the fireplace and took a saucer of milk up to her husband in the bedroom before having her own dinner with her parents, as was her custom.

Early next morning she came out of the bedroom

looking deathly pale, with tears streaming down her waxen cheeks. Her parents rushed to her, looking for the trace of a snakebite, or else strangulation marks, signs that they had pretended to banish from their minds but which in their anguish they had never ceased to fear seeing on her.

She shook her head, trying to explain what had happened, but without success. When her parents finally accepted that nothing untoward had happened to her, they at last asked her about her husband. She replied, "He has vanished." And then: "He dissolved." And lastly: "He melted away."

They went into the bedroom, looked for the snake everywhere, looked for him or for his remains, or at least his skin. Nothing to be found. They examined all the openings through which he might have gone, the windows, the door, the shutters. The night, like all nights in January, was a cold one, and everything had been shut tight. The only route by which he could have escaped was the chimney, but as the embers of the evening fire were still glowing bright, he could not imaginably have gotten out that way.

That night, and all the days and weeks that followed, the young bride, now widowed, did not offer a word of explanation. She just said over and over: He melted, he dissolved, he vanished . . . regurgitating the same phrases to the investigators and to the masters of the snake when they returned, just as somber and threatening as on their first visit.

The young woman's sorrow and the way she began to wilt soon put an end to any suspicions of an intentional disposal of the snake-husband. She was fading away with grief, in a manner not often seen in new brides. Under the black veil that she wore in accordance with the custom for widows, she looked no more than a shadow when she walked to church on Sundays. Thenceforth she was known only as "the snake's widow," but these words were said without malice, and she took no offense at them.

In the spring, her hand was asked in marriage not once but twice, and both times the proposal was rejected. It turned out to be an eventful season. Criers went out to announce in every village that the prince had resolved to outlaw from that day on any form of marriage with a beast, tree, or bird, as well as the use of pressure to make people suffer such humiliation. The word *snake* was not heard in the proclamation, but everyone knew that it was the snake business that had prompted the order — just as it raised puzzling queries about the old Code of Laws, whose mantle of authority seemed to be wearing ever thinner. It had seemed tempting very often to set down in writing the prohibition on breaking any of the rules of the Code, but the idea was eventually abandoned. It seemed like a sacrilege to write down anything about it. But then tribes that the Romans called "Slaves" poured down into the North, into the great Plain of Arberia, and that seemed an extra reason to strengthen the authority of the old *Kanun*.

In the autumn the young woman was once again asked

in marriage, and once again the request was made in vain. It turned out to be the last time anyone would ask to marry her. It became generally accepted that she had decided never to wed again.

Her decision, together with the measures taken by the prince, failed to put an end to a story that was now no longer very fresh; on the contrary, they seemed to give it new life. What in fact was the mystery that had taken place there, right before everyone's eyes? Well, they had all seen fine and famous fellows leaving widows, the sort of husbands you could not imagine being forgotten; all the same, long after the death of the great man, they had all seen the widows — with head held low and eyes full of tears, to be sure — agreeing, almost reluctantly, but agreeing all the same, to marry a second time. Whereas the snake's widow obstinately refused to do anything of the sort.

There was an intolerable enigma at the bottom of this story. Something obscure that, paradoxically, through its very absence, blinded. What had happened on that first night of marriage, the previous October? And what actually happened on the night of January 17?

There were only three wells from which a drop of the truth might possibly be drawn: the bride herself, the priest who took her confession, and the doctor. The woman's lips were sealed on the matter, the priest's even more so. The only thing that had been squeezed out of the doctor when he was in his cups concerned the bride's virginity. Like any self-respecting newlywed, she had lost it. That piece of information left everyone bewildered, as it would not have done for any other newly wedded woman.

But one fine day morbid curiosity got the upper hand. The priest and the bride had given nothing away, but something else came along to betray them. The snake's widow fell ill with a high fever, with bouts of delirious speech. And that is how she let it all out.

So this is what had really happened on that wedding night, when the household had fallen silent. The bride's parents, crossing themselves as they went, took their daughter to the threshold of the nuptial chamber, asked her once more to forgive them for the decision they had made, and then closed the door on her.

The bedroom was well heated. There were two candles that cast a faint light on each side of the bed. The snake was coiled up in a corner of the conjugal bed, quite still. With jerky, doll-like movements, the bride took off her wedding dress, lay down on the sheets, and waited. The moment that had now come seemed sometimes more, and then sometimes less, terrifying than she had imagined. Apparently, the slight inebriation she had allowed herself to suffer had slightly dulled her senses. Now she prayed only that it should all be over as quickly as possible, that the bite be like lightning, and death just as instantaneous. It was all she hoped for. Otherwise she would have to submit to the cruelest and most unimaginable ordeal: being made love to by a snake.

She continued to wait. Two or three times, she glanced at the snake, and it looked back at her. Snake's eyes, as the saying goes: even the candlelight could not brighten them. Do I please you? she wondered sadly and half ironically, feeling rancor toward the snake, toward her parents, and toward the offense that she was supposed to redeem.

In her dizzy state she imagined more than once that she had dropped off to sleep. As for the snake, he remained where he was, and seemed to be sleeping as well.

In the gap between two bouts of dozing, she thought she heard something rustle. She shivered and opened her eyes. The snake was no longer where it had been. The time had come! Holy Mother of God! Make my nightmare less hard to bear! she prayed.

She saw the snake rising ever upward at the end of the bed, swaying this way and that. Holy Virgin! she burst out in prayer once again, but at the same instant, she heard these words: "Be not afraid, I am a man."

The speckled snakeskin inflated as if by the force of an internal hurricane, and all of a sudden fell to the ground like a cloak, revealing what was indeed a man.

"Don't be afraid," he said again. "I am your husband."

"Have pity on me," she groaned.

"It's you, my wife, who should have pity on me."

He came slowly toward her, put one knee on the bed, and said soothing words to her. He was a handsome young man, with fair hair cut in the fashion of the times.

"I have been sentenced to spending three-quarters of my

life in the form of a snake," he explained. "I can live as a man for only one-quarter of the time."

The bride was bursting with questions. When was this pact made? Who had decided it? Why did you not ask for more?

Even before she had managed to put these questions into words, the man answered her:

"Nobody can know when or with whom he makes a pact. It's probably with himself."

"Do you also have an offense to atone for?"

"I have to presume I do."

She was tempted to tell him that he was even more handsome that any dream-husband she had ever imagined.

"I have only a little time left, dear soul," he said. "My hours are numbered. I have to go back to my other shape before dawn."

He drew closer to her, stroked her hair softly; then, since she wanted to smell the nape of his neck to be sure he had the smell of a human being, he let her have her way. He began to caress her breasts, kissed her on the lips, ran his mouth over her belly, telling her all the while that he had been dazzled by her beauty the very first time he had caught sight of her.

She would have liked to ask him if he thought as a human even when he was in the form of a snake, but everything suggested that it was indeed so.

He became bolder with his caresses, kissed her belly again, and then, lower down, her other lips. Now he added to his tender words stronger ones, whispering in her ear the kind of vulgarities that the village boys use on their way home from Sunday church. It was those words that won her and made her give in to him entirely.

He lay dozing at her side, in a state of exhaustion, while she stroked his blond hair. Then she too yielded to fitful sleep, but each time she came to, she glanced sideways at the snakeskin lying on the floor. What is this happiness that I feel? she wondered, fearfully.

As dawn approached, he woke up in a start. He sniffed the air and smelled sunrise coming. He declared that the time had come.

"Do not be sad. Tomorrow, at the same hour, you will have me here once again."

He threw his snakeskin over his shoulder, and in a trice he turned back into a serpent and curled himself up into a coil at the end of the bed.

She began to cry softly. But she felt so weary that she dropped off at last into a deep, deep sleep.

When she woke up, the snake was where she had last seen it. She was sure she had been dreaming. It was only when she felt the sperm in her groin and saw the bloodstains on the bed linen that she accepted that what had been, had been.

Never in her life had she looked forward to anything with as much impatience and anxiety as she felt while waiting for the next day to turn into evening and the evening to night. Now and again, as her eyes met those of the snake, her heart sank. Then she recalled the last words she had said to him together with his reply:

"You really will come, you won't let me down?"

"I shall come, I promise. Wait for me."

The word of a snake! she thought, then repented having had such a thought.

He did indeed reappear in his human shape, around midnight. And so, day after day, night after night, all through the autumn, the onset of winter, and through to the darkest days of the bad season, she lived such an undreamed-of, double life. A life in which time itself was cleft in two — the rarest of all wonders. She was henceforth obliged to live in two different kinds of time — human time and reptilian time. Because of this, every point of view was distorted, like the view in a broken mirror. People pitied her, thought she was at her wits' end, whereas she had never been so happy in her life. She had heard it said that it was very hard to mask one's own suffering, but she found that hiding her happiness was no less burdensome. She tried as hard as she could, but she did not succeed.

People assumed she had gone mad. Anyway, it seemed almost reasonable for a woman to lose her wits after a shock like that. That did not bother her. What pained her most of all was that she could not walk out on her husband's arm, as all young brides did, during his human time. It was forbidden: the pact prevented him from doing it. He was only allowed out with her during his snake time.

That was how the pact had been drawn up. Snake time ruled for three-quarters of his existence. Human time was restricted to the remainder, and moreover was not allowed to be shown. But that was only natural, as it was a matter of redeeming a human offense in this strange way.

She knew all that, of course, but her knowledge did not stop her dreaming of the opposite: going out with him, arm in arm, to the village square, walking with him to church for Sunday service. And her desire for these things was sometimes so overpowering that she found herself on the point of going out with the snake, forgetting entirely that people were likely to take fright when they saw them and flee.

One day she asked him if he would like to go out with her in his snake shape, for a walk along some deserted path, but he shrugged his shoulders. As a human he knew nothing of the part of the day when he was a snake. In addition he had no right to know anything about it, just as his other self could not intervene in his life as a man. He and I, he told her, are separate in every sense.

These thoughts troubled her constantly, but on that fateful night of January 17, her irritation at having to keep a secret, her weariness at leading a double life, and her desire to have her young husband for herself and for all of the time condensed in her mind like steam turning into water.

It is past midnight. As usual, the couple have made love,

and he is dozing with his head on her shoulder. In the light of the glowing embers in the fireplace, she is looking at his hair and at the fine contour of his cheek. Then her eyes wander toward the thin skin left lying on the floor, its scales seeming to shine with a special light. It seems to her that the snakeskin is laughing at her, with malice.

She keeps staring at the outer coil. That is the real obstacle, she thinks. That is where separation, cleavage, and the forbidden frontier all lie. It is as thin as the coat of blacking that turns glass into a mirror, it is just as fragile and just as cruel.

And what if it was all a misunderstanding? What if the young man had been caught in a pact without reason?

She must free him from his trap, from the snare that consumes him a little more every day. If she can only manage to smash the bewitching mirror, then the young man won't be able to get away, whether he wants to or not. He'll stay on this side, and be hers entirely.

You brought me all this woe, and now you have the cheek to laugh at me? she says to the snakeskin. You've got another think coming!

So as not to wake her sleeping lover, she gets out of bed slowly and carefully, and for the first time in her life feels the touch of the snakeskin. It seems to her unbelievably light, lighter even than silk; there's good reason, she thinks, to put snakeskin alongside gauze.

Suddenly her eyes narrow in anger. You have no right!

she screams inwardly. "You" means the whole world — her parents, the pact, those who drew up the pact, all the other mysterious forces, and fate itself.

With a swift movement of her arm, she throws the snakeskin into the hearth. She has never seen anything devoured so hungrily by fire. The merest instant suffices. The tiniest fragment of time.

She sneaks back to bed as quietly and discreetly as possible. He is still asleep. She feels relieved and burdened at the same time, as if she had just lifted a rock.

And so she waits for daybreak. Dawn comes. The young man stretches his limbs and sniffs the morning air. She is about to say, Sleep on a little, now that you belong to the other time. But she cannot.

He says what he usually does: "Farewell, until tomorrow. Do not be downcast, dear soul."

He gets out of bed and starts looking this way and that. "Where is my suit?"

The bride does not answer.

"Have you hidden it? Please don't play games!"

He searches for it everywhere, anxiously looking into every nook and cranny, under the blankets, everywhere.

"I am in a hurry. Give me back my snake suit."

"I cannot," she replies.

He keeps on searching like a man possessed. "Mercy!" he mumbles now and again.

She pretends to be angry. "Don't you want to stay with

me? Are you in such a hurry to go?" But in fact, it is not anger but fear that she feels.

"Stay!" she cries out, but her voice sticks in her throat. "Calm down! Stay on this side. . . ."

"I cannot. I no longer have a shape. . . . I have no right. . . ."

His voice gets weaker. He strains for breath between each word.

"I beg you, give me back my suit."

"I cannot, I have burned it."

"What did you do?" he yells, but his yell now sounds as though it comes from far away. "You have killed me, by your own hand!"

"I did it for you. And for both of us."

"You have destroyed me. . . ."

It is his last gasp. Like breath that has misted on a mirror, the young man fades away before his bride's eyes, and then vanishes entirely, and forever.

With a kind of passionate intensity that had recently become almost normal for him, Mark Gurabardhi ran through the entire range of suppositions that must have surfaced after that night of January 17. It was almost as if he had himself taken part in the interrogation that the bride, her parents, and her neighbors were put through.

First hypothesis: the snake had been put to death. Had the young woman thrown the snake — not just the skin, but the reptile itself — into the fire? Unaided? Or with the help of her parents? Isn't that how they had sought to expunge the stain that had been visited on them in full public knowledge, even if it involved taking a risk? (Isn't it true that many people, in like manner, overcome by despair, rip the signs of humiliation from their clothes or from their doors?)

Second issue: the girl's seeming delight on the morning after her wedding night. It could be accounted for if she had been given an assurance (by a parent or clansman) that the abomination would not last long.

Next: the loss of her virginity. There were so many ways to lose it in the overcrowded intimacy of large families, where brothers, sisters, and cousins of both sexes all lived under the same roof!

The only element that was incompatible with this version of the story lay in the visible and profound decline of the bride after the disappearance of the snake. It was a real and apparently unremitting affliction. And this awkward fact obliged everybody to try to develop an alternative hypothesis.

Was it a dream? Had the girl had a hallucination? That could not be ruled out. Everybody had seen the snake, whereas nobody had seen the young man. It was thus perfectly possible that, putting aside any attempt to escape the public humiliation, the whole development of the story — the young man's good looks, his irrepressible passion, etc. — had been the mere imaginings of a young bride under unbearable stress.

Mark's hands reached for a pack of cigarettes in one pocket as quickly as he would have reached for his revolver if he had had to defend himself against a mugger.

And what if neither explanation was right? A drama usually exists less in reality than in the fertile mind of its inventor. In those days, disappointment on a wedding night was just about the commonest, most everyday tragedy you could imagine: the partner might have been horribly ugly, or infirm, or impotent. . . . It was an ancient tragedy, one that went back to the times when people in the millions accepted marriage without ever having set eyes upon their spouse. That world was being reinvented now, by the Internet.

Mark smiled inwardly. Then he felt his smile vanish. How can I explain the fear I feel? he wondered.

He was afraid, and he was cold. He tried to banish all these old questions from his mind, but nothing could have been more difficult. . . .

To take things one step further, if you made an effort to think from inside the legend, it told of an encounter between man and beast at a special moment when they were facing each other in a place where they should not have been together. Both had overstepped the boundary and ended up merged into a single body, in a temporal order that belonged to neither one nor the other. Yes, that's how they managed to kill each other so brutally.

So that's how things really happened, Mark surmised, and again he felt pierced by the cold. All the time I've wasted these last months constructing crazy hypotheses about snakes! . . .

He suddenly thought back, with what he considered to be amazing clarity, to that summer's afternoon when, in their drab Tirana apartment, his stern-faced father had tried to persuade him to enroll at the Police Academy instead of the School of Fine Arts.

His father stared at him hard with his one good eye, projecting a flood of grumpy bitterness. He had long been aware that his father's one eye (the other had been lost in a shoot-out with bandits) could express joy and sorrow in alternation. You're refusing to do the only thing I've ever asked of you! was what the reproachful one-eyed gaze seemed to be saying. You couldn't tell whether his father's main reason was his belief in law and order or his desire to avenge the loss of his eye.

"You'll wear a police uniform, just like me, just like your grandfather, who was murdered by brigands under the monarchy."

"No, Father. I won't be wearing that uniform. . . ."

Mark's mind resumed its drift: uniform . . . suit . . . snakeskin. . . . Whereupon he cried out loud: "I must stop this!"

CHAPTER 2

THE ONLY SUBJECT OF CONVERSATION all over town that
Sunday afternoon was the holdup at the bank. A rumor
spread that the outlaws had been captured at Mountain
Springs, but it turned out to be unfounded. The caretaker,
though, who had been found with his hands and wrists tied
up, provided some information about the robbers: there
were three of them, they'd worn masks, and they were
armed. It still wasn't known by what means they had managed to force the safe. Nor how much they had gotten away
with.

Mark Gurabardhi looked for Zef high and low, to get
more of the story out of him, but the man was nowhere to
be found. He wasn't at home or in the pool hall. As Mark
watched the lights go out in the windows one by one, he
realized with some surprise that he was fascinated by the

incident, as was the whole town, but maybe even more than anyone else. As a rule, he was usually much less interested than other people in local events like football matches or political meetings. He didn't really know whether his relative indifference was to his advantage or not. But if up to now he had been vaguely proud of not being like most ordinary folk, should he not now feel diminished by being part of the common herd?

He shook his head as if to rid it of this idiotic worry. Whether he was ashamed of it or not, he was a human being like any other, as curious as the next man about what happens on Earth: about how banks can be robbed, about how turtles make love, about how sick kings in the Middle Ages were cleaned after they had relieved themselves. (Ever since the director of the City Arts Center had gotten back from Spain two weeks before and had told him about the sad end of Philip II at the Escorial Palace, Mark could not get that last image out of his mind.)

As he went back into his apartment, he stopped at the door to look at it carefully, especially the lock, and then closed it carelessly behind him. There was nothing to steal here. Except, perhaps, the portrait of his young mistress, which he had hung on the wall over the head of the bed. He stretched out, folded his hands behind his head, and stared at the ceiling, hoping that this would help to empty his mind completely.

Sundown, on a Sunday, in the back of beyond . . . he soon began to dream. Doubly desolate, after making love.

He would gladly have swapped one of his lovemaking sessions (even the second orgasm, which had been the better) for an hour with his girlfriend in the café, in the evening.

He hoped that new ways and manners would quickly take hold in his little town of B——. After all, B—— was in Albania, too! Everything's connected! he often thought. He could not understand how, in other towns, white slavers sending girls to work as prostitutes in Italy were uncovered every day, whereas here in B—— girls didn't even dare spend an hour in the café with their boyfriends.

But he had not lost hope, and that was one of the reasons why he had not tried very hard to get transferred to Tirana when the dictatorship had taken its first major battering.

He was tempted to smile at the thought that it was barely a few years since his graduation from the School of Fine Arts and his appointment to this northern town, where, in the eyes of all the local girls, he had been the very embodiment of modernity. Because in some incomprehensible way the tables had suddenly been turned. Nowadays, between two embraces, his girlfriend would tell him, You know, there's a new fashion in this or that. He didn't feel mortally offended, no, he had almost come to savor the process of being aged, even though he was not yet thirty. To begin with, without really realizing what he was doing, he'd encouraged her to take on this new role as his guide; eventually, he grasped that what he really wanted was for her to become his Beatrice, to lead him through purgatory.

He had become so inured to this feeling that he reckoned

that when the day came, she would say to him, Come on, it's time go out to the café, and he would trust her command, blindly, almost superstitiously, and would follow her without the slightest hesitation.

Without moving his head, he rolled his eyes upward, as he sometimes did, to look at her portrait. From this obtuse angle, she looked quite different, especially the top of her face. The slant of her eyes, which now seemed to suggest some elegant deception, matched and complemented the change he had noticed under her arms. But like everything else late that Sunday afternoon, that suspicion was devoid of pain.

He thought of the table waiting for him in that dingy little restaurant, and then of his walk home through the town, when, despite all the excitement aroused by the holdup of the bank, lights would go out in the apartments and houses, one after the other, at exactly the same time as on any other Sunday.

As people went back to work and offices reopened, Mondays would bring their own corrections to Sunday's gossip about every little weekend scandal and event. In the old days, the phenomenon was easily accounted for. In fear of the State, people altered their opinions to fit what they heard from official sources. By the same token, their own explanations were often quite divergent. A suicide for thwarted love? It was reckoned that something deeper was involved. Or conversely, that such and such a quarrel had no political motive at all, but was just a spat between sisters-in-law.

In the early days of the new era, people no longer gave a penny for official opinion, as they became free, from one day to the next, to adopt the opposite point of view. But to their great surprise, no significant change occurred. As in the past, once they got home from work, they would hear about events in such a mangled way that the stories were often completely distorted. Gradually, it became clear that, as for many other things, such distortions of the truth had nothing to do with politics. Apparently, for reasons still not understood, rumor, vivified over the weekend by the smells of good food and Grandma's burps, had a hard time when it first encountered the atmosphere of the office, the clacking of typewriters, the secretaries' lipstick, and, last but not least, the stern gaze of the boss.

Even if you could never say that the office had won out completely (as soon as people got home, they had to negotiate the mule-like persistence of grandmas, often reinforced by the children just back from school), even if, in this constant ebb and flow of home and office, office and home, rumor was never quite exempt from further shaping before it settled down into its definitive form, the first major impact on it, what might be called "the Monday spin," was always the principal determining factor.

That was all going through Mark's head as he walked

toward the City Arts Center, where he worked. The music section head's office door, next to his own, was ajar, and voices could be heard from within. He opened it wider, and even before he was actually inside, the words "safe" and "gangsters" reached his ears.

"Morning," he said. "Have the robbers been caught?"

"No, not yet," the head of music answered. "The director was just telling us about a bank holdup that took place in Madrid while he was there."

"Oh, sorry to interrupt."

"No, not at all, you're not interrupting us, Mark," the director said.

He was still wearing a white shirt with a "Boss" logo on the front, and his sky blue tie made his smile even more radiant.

He's not finished boring the whole place with tales of his trip to Spain, Mark said to himself.

Even so, he didn't dislike the man. Quite the opposite, in fact. There was something touching about the way his face expressed sheer joy at the memory of the jaunt that had, apparently, turned his life upside down. The sunny feelings that he had experienced over there suited him to a tee, just like his saying "No problem!" It was the most common expression these days in the whole ex-Communist empire, and it seemed to have been coined especially for him.

The director looked at his watch.

"Okay, you guys, let's go into my office for a moment to get this concert straight."

This was surely one of the most exhilarating moments of the day for the director: moving down the corridor with his posse of underlings, as straight-backed as any rising executive, casting words of greeting and cheer to left and right.

On this occasion things took their habitual course, except that the director refrained from saying "Okay." His office was littered with souvenirs from Spain, but Mark was convinced — he would have sworn to it — that not a soul felt any resentment or even the slightest condescension toward the director. Professionally inclined toward harmony, Mark had long thought that there was a perfect match between the director's harmless vanity and pet expressions, on the one hand, and the elegance of his wife, who dressed as carefully as he did, and who had opened the first ladies' hairdressing salon in B——, and the way the couple complemented each other so well had quite extinguished any animosity he might have felt toward his boss.

Sometimes Mark seemed to read in the director's eyes a silent question: So why don't you share my enthusiasm? A new era has begun, what's stopping you from enjoying it?

So what *is* stopping us? Mark wondered when he got back to his own office. Obviously he didn't know, or rather, he didn't want to know.

He puttered around for a while between his desk and his window, picked up the telephone to make sure the line was connected, then went out.

"If anyone wants to get hold of me, tell them I've gone back to the studio," he told his secretary.

Once he got outside, he did not follow the avenue of lindens that led to his studio, but instead turned left. All the shops were open. He stopped in front of a low shack. There was a sign outside: "Kol Koleci — Keys and Locks."

"I thought I'd be seeing you," said the craftsman.

"Oh, did you? And why so?"

The shopkeeper gave a vulgar laugh.

"How, why? As soon as people have got two pennies to rub together, they beat a path to my door. And you . . ."

"Really, so why me? You know I don't have any money."

"Yes, I know you haven't got a dollar to your name. But you're a painter. And there's no one who knows better than you how much your Mona Lisas are worth. That's what you call valuable paintings, isn't it?"

"Ho, ho!" Mark burst out laughing. "You think I could be burgled?"

"In the old days, no. But nowadays, yes," the locksmith replied. "In the old days, they didn't even bother to rob banks!"

"By the way, have you heard anything more about that? Have they nabbed the robbers?"

"Not yet," the locksmith replied. "Not yet," he repeated a moment later. "There's a heap of unanswered questions. How did they manage to smash the outer gate without the caretaker hearing? How did they manage to tie him up? Not to mention how they managed to penetrate the safe, and the essential question: Where is their hideout? But let's come back to what brings you here. I guess it's for your studio?"

Mark nodded. He tried to explain what was wrong with

his door, but the locksmith interrupted him: "I'd better go see for myself."

He looked for a pencil, scrawled "Back in half an hour" on a piece of paper, and pinned it to his door. Then he followed Mark on his way.

During the walk, the locksmith kept coming back to his suspicions about the bank heist. Where did these crooks in balaclavas come from? Up in these mountains, no one had ever worn masks.

Mark was tempted to reply that maybe the robbers came from somewhere far away, but his eyes had wandered to the window of a new shop, and he stopped to look.

"Well, well," he said as he almost read aloud the words on the shopfront: "SILVANA SALON DE COIFFURE. *Shampoo — Coloring — Permanent Wave*. It's the wife of the director of the Arts Center."

"Really?" the locksmith said. "You didn't know she had opened her shop?"

"I'd been told. Of course, I had heard, but . . ."

The locksmith nodded his head and smiled.

"He comes to collect his wife here almost every evening after work. When you see him, all dressed up and looking so pleased with himself, it's hard to remember he's a local lad, a mountain boy. He looks like he comes straight from the capital. Oh, you're frowning, I know what you're going to answer, that there are plenty of ragamuffins in Tirana as well. I know that as well as you, but for us, all the same, the capital means something! And anyway, our mountain areas are going to be modernized as well, aren't they? They'll also get civilized, like people say these days, and that's a fact!"

"Sure," Mark replied. "No doubt about it, Kol."

They were now quite close to the studio, and slowed their pace.

As they went up the stairs, Mark felt that the locksmith's expression had changed. His eyes had become alternately intense and haughty. They lit up as soon as he saw a door, and went dull whenever they were directed toward anything else. The eye of a true craftsman, Mark thought. He didn't even bother to turn the nude portrait of his girlfriend to the wall, as he usually did when he had visitors in the studio.

The locksmith hurried about the studio, huffing and puffing, from one corner to another, as if he were trying to find cover from a potential threat.

Mark could not take his eyes off him. He sought but could not find on the locksmith's face some reading of the extent of the danger, for he was sure that in the craftsman's mind the danger was proportionate to the value of the paintings. As he tracked the man's stops and starts, and the sporadic glints in his eye, Mark felt as though he were await-ing a sentence. Did the locksmith believe, or did he not, that the studio was at risk of being burgled?

Talking more to himself than to his client, in one spot the locksmith mumbled, "This lock'll have to be changed," and at another, "Well, these door panels need strengthening, for sure," "You'll need a vertical bolt right here," "Both sides of the jamb need metal catches. . . ."

The inspection went on. At one point, Mark tried to interrupt with additional information, but what he got by way of response was silent fury. The locksmith's eyes, divided by a deep vertical furrow right down his forehead, suddenly turned threatening.

"Look, do you want to be safe . . . or be burgled?"

Mark blushed to the nape of his neck, something that did not happen to him often.

"Sorcerer!" he muttered to himself. How had the man managed to see into the depths of his soul?

He took comfort in the thought that the locksmith's state of overexcitement meant that the man would have forgotten the exchange entirely in a few days' time.

The scene was brought to an end, so it seemed, by a deep sigh from the craftsman. He suddenly went limp; in an instant, his eyes lost their sparkle and also the look of contempt with which they had been filled. He cast about for something to sit on.

"Would you like a drink?" asked Mark.

The locksmith had turned back into an ordinary human, and his breathing had resumed a normal rhythm.

"Theft can explain how the whole world goes round," he said as he lit a cigarette. "You can tell a man by his looks, people say. I have a very different opinion."

He was talking once again in his natural voice, with his customary jocular intonation. It wasn't the way someone behaved, or spoke, or wrote or drew, according to him, that best defined what sort of a person he or she was —

especially as far as amorous relations were concerned —
but above all the way he or she forced a lock. It was a surer
mark of a rapist than any sample of blood or sperm. And
the same thing went for sodomists.

Mark began to laugh out loud. His eye caught the canvas
of the nude, but now it was too late to turn it to the wall.
Anyway, as the girl's face was still unfinished, she remained
quite unidentifiable.

"That's how burglars and burgled alike give themselves
away," the locksmith continued. "Thieves, as I said, can be
identified by the way they break locks, and their victims can
be recognized by their choice of locks. You could sum up a
whole epoch by its locks and bolts — or rather, by its styles
of breaking and entering."

He got off his chair and wandered around the studio.
Mark thought he was now looking at the paintings with another kind of eye.

"This one, I don't know, it looks different from the others. Is it by you?"

Mark smiled.

"It's a copy of a painting by a great Spanish master, a
painter called El Greco. I did it as a learning exercise, at
college."

"Oh, I see."

On his return from Spain, the director had told him
about Philip II's retreat to the Escorial, and ever since then,
Mark could not look at his old exercise without imagining

the sick man's gloomy chamber, where few people stayed very long, apart from his sisters, because of the stink.

"There used to be quite extraordinary heists," the locksmith said. "My father — may his soul rest in peace — taught me my trade, and told me a whole mess of good stories." He chuckled under his breath, as if hesitating to say out loud what had just come into his mind. "Did you ever imagine anyone could steal a coffin?"

"No, I've heard stories about corpses being stolen, but never about a stolen coffin."

"Well, then. One of our neighbors got his wife's coffin pinched! In those days, I suppose you remember, it was the custom to have coffins delivered well ahead of the funeral, and to stand them up, empty, like they were on show, by the front door of the bereaved. Well, then. It got pinched. The poor old husband seemed to have lost his wits. Then his despair suddenly turned into joy. He reckoned it was a good omen. He got so taken up with the idea that he convinced himself his wife wasn't dead, and he started shaking her like she was an apple tree, to make her come to!"

"Unbelievable!" the painter exclaimed politely.

"At one time there were bandits aplenty on the Shkodër road," the locksmith said after a pause. "As well as up the Tepelen Gorge, and farther on, all the way to Janina."

He talked about thieving as others would talk of a drought, of an especially heavy snowfall, or of an unusually bountiful harvest.

"Under the dictatorship, robberies, like everything else, shrank to nothing. But it's getting late."

He stood up, and then rattled off in two minutes the list of all the equipment he needed and the time it would take to complete the job, not forgetting, of course, his estimate of the charge.

Mark walked him back to the shop and then returned to the studio to look at the items that the locksmith said needed strengthening. Then he walked up and down, as he always did when he felt preoccupied. As he came up to the Greco copy, he thought that he too would like to be looked after by his sisters. As for his girlfriend, he would certainly like her by his bedside, but . . . only if he were injured!

He wondered how such an idea had lodged itself in his head. He stared for a moment at the corner of the bay window. He didn't know why, but he vaguely imagined that that was where the bullet meant for him would come from.

Maybe he ought to take that picture down? At least until his boss had got tired of talking about his trip to Spain.

He couldn't get his mind off what the locksmith had just told him about robberies. It was as if in the locksmith's mind that was the principal approach to understanding world history. Just as some people had tried to explain history exclusively in terms of the role of women.

Banditry flourished from the very start of the monarchy, he thought in a daze, going over the locksmith's account. All the same his eye kept going back to that spot on the windowpane through which, he imagined, a bullet could get him. The fantasy grew so powerful that he ended up imagining the lead slug fluttering around the studio like a trapped bird.

The Voskopoja painters, he dreamed, would perhaps be the first to paint his portrait. . . . Painting a wound is easier than almost anything else. But what a lot of nonsense! he thought. He'd better have a little rest. Talking to that locksmith had left him completely drained, so it seemed. All that great sea of thieving . . . So much murderous criminality, he wanted to say.

Two or three times he wondered why he had found the subject so affecting. But his brain was drawn toward evil, so to speak, and was rushing headlong in the wrong direction. He wasn't often given to such mental ramblings; maybe he was having a bout of fever. He was aware that if that was so, the best thing was to offer no resistance. . . . He should just let himself go until he was exhausted, let himself sink to the bottom of the sea of dreams. . . .

Nonetheless he felt a shiver, just as he had done a few days previously. His recently rediscovered fascination with police work was an ill wind. . . . All this cop stuff . . . He recalled once again that awful afternoon with his father, when they had quarreled over his choice of career. That look in his father's eye. That lonely look in a police officer's face . . . Mark, said his instructor, what is this peculiar drawing? It's nothing, sir, nothing at all, I don't know what came over me. . . .

Mark's father had given way in the end, but the afternoon

of their quarrel had left deep scars. Or rather, it had implanted a kind of hidden virus that flared up in a bout of fever every now and again. After the Fourth Artists' Plenum, just before the arrest of Gentian, he repented the choice he had made. The other choice, working for the police, however humiliating it might have been, was the only other path he had ever considered following. And for that reason it was the only career he ever thought of as his unrealized potential.

Later, when the TV news came on, with items on left-wing and right-wing demonstrators fighting hand to hand with the forces of law and order, he could not rid his mind of the thought that at that very moment on the screen it could have been him out there, down in the square. . . .

For some time now he had felt constrained by this second life, parallel to the one he was leading. He smiled about it, to be sure, but he had to wonder how high he would have risen by now if he had joined the police. Maybe he would be an assistant chief of police in some desolate backwater just like this one.

Two days before, when he had heard the story of the now-famous holdup of the National Bank, he had caught himself grinning, just as a rake who hears talk of women prides himself on being the expert in the field.

He was both ashamed and jubilant. No matter: he felt that he had jumped, of his own accord, into a pool of inanity, and could no longer climb out. His attitude was that of an obligation toward his second life, rather as he might feel obligated toward a long-abandoned girlfriend.

In recent times his second life — which for so many years had existed as a silent parallel — had not, as anticipated, dwindled to nothing but rather had seemed to reassert itself ever more firmly. It sometimes weighed upon him so much that he imagined that his police uniform was right there, waiting for him. At the back of the studio he had an old chest that he was afraid to open because he feared his uniform was already inside it.

It was no accident that the Gentian affair and the story of the snakeskin had both had such a strong impact on him.

He had presumably gotten himself tangled up in one of those gauzelike webs that lie in wait almost everywhere, but which people of normal sensitivity are unable to see or feel. Maybe he would get free of the sticky threads when the time came (a time long ago determined) for his parallel life as a policeman to be cut short, scythed by a gangster's bullet.

Then he would feel free, that's for sure.

Sometimes he told himself to be thankful: at least he didn't have to cope with a third or a fourth life! He didn't dare broach the subject with his girlfriend, afraid she would think him out of his mind. All the same, he imagined talking it over with her: You're lucky not to be afraid of that, he might say. You know, there are people who, for one reason or another, maybe just because things turned out that way, come up to the surface, as if they were climbing out of a deep hole, after they've been lost . . . how can I say . . . in another universe, in a different system. Just as it must be with black holes in space. Can you imagine coming to the edge of a black hole? Time slows down, then comes to a stop. . . . But then, at that point, when you've fallen in, you reappear in a different space . . . a different system . . . a new state of being. . . . Obviously no one has actually been inside a black hole . . . except that snake in the old legend.

He had another nightmare, that of seeing millions of people taking leave of their own lives, in some general decomposition of the universe, so as to take possession of others; but he managed to keep that mad fear at bay. Pythagoras must surely have thought about it carefully, but, in sheer horror, had never described it anywhere.

In the context of such impending chaos, his own tumbling fall into a second life sometimes seemed no more than natural to him. As did his fascination with unsolved mysteries. With the secret of the pyramids, for instance. He had always been curious about the pillaging of the pyramids. But such things were relatively close at hand, located in the suburbs of human history. The thefts of biblical times were more distant, and beyond them, after a yawning chasm of time, the celestial region began. That was where the really great plundering must have taken place: maybe even the mother of all burglaries, or at any rate, the essence of theft.

You're off your rocker! he told himself But that didn't stop him from summoning up the image of Prometheus as he had drawn him at the School of Fine Arts, scuttling away from Mount Olympus with fire clutched under his cloak. His instructor had pulled a long face at the drawing: That's not Prometheus, lad! That's just a common pickpocket!

The locksmith was probably right. Civilization began with a robbery. Yet it was a fact that no one wanted to acknowledge. Out of shame, presumably; or maybe not?

Mark jumped off the bed and went to the shelf where he kept his books. He leafed through the *Dictionary of Mythology,* to P . . . Pr . . . Pro . . . Prometheus. His quarrel with Zeus . . . the theft of fire. Aha! he cried. The theft of fire was the second robbery carried out on Olympus. The first was the theft of immortality.

He browsed through the pages and ended up finding what he was looking for. It seemed he had always known this, but maybe he had forgotten it in the meanwhile. He drank in these few lines once, then again, shaking his head, not fully satisfied. It was obscure and poorly explained, like a ruined building in the dark. That's what accounted for his lapse of memory.

Under the thief's name, Tantalus, he found nothing further. A theft committed on a dark night . . . the proof of immortality implemented through a mortal. Tantalus caught in flagrante delicto. The punishment he suffered . . .

Seen from a great distance, the two events that took place in the heavens seemed almost simultaneous. But if you look more closely, you see that the scandal of immortality was prior to the theft of fire. To be sure, they were closer together than, say, the pillaging of the pyramids and the holdup at the bank of B——. That's why he had lost his grasp of it all. Nonetheless, in the fire business, some of the circumstances were known: Prometheus's visit to the workshop of Hephaistos, where fire was kept, the seizure of a burning coal or torch, the flight over the earth with his booty hidden in his breast, and the gift that he made of it to men. But absolutely nothing was known about the theft of immortality: neither when nor where it had happened; in what shape it was held to exist; how it could have come to be stolen, and, in the event, transported by its thief. . . .

He shook his head again and again. No, the event had not been rubbed out by forgetting. It was just that it had never been properly explained. The human mind had stopped short on the threshold of the mystery. The mind that gives way to no obstacle, had, in this instance, recognized its own impotence. It had gone too far, come too close to the frozen wastes at the very frontier of the impossible, and had been forced to turn back.

With his hands clasped at the back of his neck as if they were needed to hold his head up straight to withstand the shock, Mark recalled the fragments of the myth of the theft of immortality. One pitch-black night, a messenger of Death knocks at the door of a thoroughly ordinary mortal. "Who goes there?" To which Death's emissary gives his customary reply: "Open up, I am the envoy of Death." From behind the closed door, the mortal answers: "Go back whence thou came, I have nothing to do with you."

Mark smiled to himself. He hadn't indulged in such idle

dreams for a long while. He had even felt hurt by imagining himself no longer capable of such reveries. Lazily, in the way you sip and savor a delicious summer drink, he tried to reconstruct the smallest details of the long-buried event. But something was stopping him. He got up, paced up and down the room, looked out of his bay window at the poplars lining the street, then at the low clouds, and he realized that a different story had woven itself in his mind into the one he was trying to recall. You thought you had become a great painter, didn't you? You thought you had become an immortal artist, like people say, and so you wouldn't have anything to do with us anymore? Isn't that what you thought?

That's what the interrogator had said to Gentian, and what Gentian had reported to him as soon as they let him out of prison. If he were to live a thousand years, Mark knew that he would never snuff out the memory of his terror during that stifling summer in Tirana. Gentian hadn't yet been hauled in, but the threat was palpable, hovering in the air. As soon as the Fourth Plenum was over, there had been meetings all the time at the Writers' and Artists' Union. The heat was unbearable, and for some reason Mark imagined that it would somehow help to mitigate the disaster. Maybe the authorities would remember that holidays and beaches and seasides also existed. And if they had forgotten, then their wives and children would remind them. So maybe they would put off all those meetings until September.

But no, nobody seemed to be thinking of ordinary life that summer. Quite the opposite: yet more sessions were planned. Some of them were to be closed sessions. Others were to be public hearings. And yet others half open and half closed. They all seemed to be the same, and yet they weren't. People also whispered about extra-special meetings that were to be declared to have taken place when they hadn't, and others that would really be held but would be said to have never happened.

Whenever he heard rumors of this kind, Mark put them down initially to the mental muddle fostered by the psychotic atmosphere of the times, but on second thought, they seemed to be perfectly coherent assumptions. It was obvious that not everybody would be summoned to appear at public meetings, and that closed sessions would be designed to allow fear-inducing rumors to leak out. Otherwise, what was the point?

He was almost certain that his turn would come, after Gentian's. Once his friend's flat had been searched and his paintings confiscated by the police, Mark fully expected he would be arrested in short order. He felt the same terror when other painters were summoned to appear before the tribunal to give evidence against the suspect. Later on, Gentian told him that in all there had been twenty-six witnesses for the prosecution. After the regular informers, who had amended their statements two or three times each, they had summoned quality witnesses, people who had not yet been "grilled," which showed how important the case against Gentian was considered. Then they called the officials of the Writers' and Artists' Union themselves, then the officials of the Art Museum, then the café waiters from both places, then one of Gentian's neighbors, who happened to be a veteran of the national liberation struggle of '45, then the girls who had posed nude for him, and last of all they heard testimony from local prostitutes. "Gentian asked me to shave the hair on both sides of my pubic area because, apparently, it is the fashion in the West." "Vermin! Cardsharp!" the magistrate yelled at the painter. That insult took Gentian by surprise, who hardly had time to reflect on the model's turpitude. He'd never played cards, and he took the magistrate's outburst as a random taunt — but a few days later, when they began to confront him with notorious gamblers, he guessed that a new case was being prepared even while the initial charges against him were being maintained. On some days he was questioned about the decadent nature of his canvases, and on other days about his newfound vice of gambling. He supposed they would eventually decide under which of the two heads he was to be judged, but the magistrates kept on switching from one to the other. Apparently they were waiting for an order from above. The decision would hang on various external factors, maybe on international relations, or the discovery of new oil fields, or even on the next annual report of Amnesty International.

"You thought you had become an immortal painter and would thus have nothing more to do with us? So you started gambling, you need money that badly?"

Mark got up in a start and went back to leafing through his dictionary of mythology. He stared at the one illustration that went with the text, an image of Tantalus in his eternal suffering. Above and beneath him, but just out of his reach, were water to slake his thirst and apples to quell his hunger. A strange sentence, quite inappropriate to the incomparably more serious crime that he had committed. It looked more like the punishment of a glutton who had allowed his fellow men to go hungry and thirsty.

True enough, it's always the same old story, Mark thought. Maybe Tantalus also had two cases against him? In the end, Gentian had been found guilty of decadent tendencies in his art, but the vice of gambling was also mentioned in an appendix to the main charge. It seems that Tantalus had had the opposite result. Since it couldn't be entirely erased, the theft of immortality had been tacked on as a minor count, to be taken into consideration. Anyway, there was no proof, no testimony about it. That had presumably been done to rub it out more easily later, since it would be held to have been a charge unproven — a mere supposition, maybe just an optical illusion. The theft of immortality was to be erased from the memory of men as from the memory of the gods.

Mark lay down again. Somehow or other he felt that in order to imagine the most mysterious event in the history of the universe, which is what he was now sure it was, he would have to be physically absent, on the outside, so to speak, in some kind of exile.

Once again his mind turned to the messenger of Death looking, in the jet-black night, for a door to knock on.

COUNTER-CHAPTER 2

IN THE PITCH-DARK NIGHT the messenger of Death knocks at a man's door. To the challenge of "Who goes there?" comes the traditional reply: "Open up, I am the messenger of Death." From behind the closed door the man shouts out, "Be on your way, you have no business here!"

The envoy scowls. He supposes that the mortal has not grasped just who he is, that the mortal has mistaken him for the tax collector or for a bailiff. And as the mortal who lives there has paid his taxes and has no quarrel with the law, he reckons the visitor has no business with him. So the envoy must knock again, and speak his words a second time, but to his amazement, from behind the closed door, the same answer comes: "Go back whence thou came, I have nothing to do with thee."

The messenger stands rooted to the ground, quite

bewildered. It's the first time anything like this has happened. Preparing himself to knock on the door for the third time, he pulls the death warrant out of his satchel, checks the mortal's name as well as the date and exact time set down for his passage into the other world — in fact, the man should have been gone from life to death for some time already, yet he is still alive and kicking. The messenger is incensed, and knocks a third time.

No answer comes from behind the door. Suddenly the door swings open, and there stands the man on the threshold. What he says is as incomprehensible as it is disturbing: "Go tell your mistress Death that I do not recognize her writ."

Upon which he flashes some trinket or other . . . well, nobody has ever discovered exactly what it was, but it must have been something like a secret medallion or cipher, an emblem or credit card number, the seal of some sect or the badge of some club, maybe even a visa that allows you to cross a border unimpeded.

The messenger of Death stands there stock-still, wide-eyed and struck dumb. Perhaps it is the first time he has ever seen that sign or symbol, but he recognizes its power and yields to it. Anyway, he is no more than a messenger, and his mission is only what he has been told to do: gather up souls. He does not even think to ask why the talisman has been entrusted to a mere mortal. All the same, since it is the first time in thousands of years that he has come across an incident of the kind, he feels duty-bound to report it to his superiors.

So he decides to alert his boss. He too is shaken by the incident, takes advice from another colleague — necessarily one more highly placed than he is — and then the two of them pluck up their courage and go to wake up Erebus, the Minister of Death himself.

Erebus can't believe his ears. "Have you taken leave of your senses?" he screams.

He adds, almost instantly, "That just about does it!" And off he goes to wake the great leader of them all, Hades.

He knows it won't be easy. He hasn't done it in the last six thousand years, at least. Especially as Hades has just wedded the sweet Persephone. That all flashes through his mind in an instant. But he does not dither or dally. Using a secret method he alone knows, he wakes the great leader.

What he hears from a distant Hades is much the same as what he had thrown back to his subordinates: "Erebus, are you in possession of all your senses, or have you lost your wits entirely?"

So Erebus has to repeat word for word all that he just said. A long silence follows. Erebus thinks with sadness of his leader's unseeing eyes. Then the latter says, "Come straight on down to see me."

When he gets there, Erebus finds the entire Bureau of Death assembled. The mines are darker than they have ever been. The black sockets of Hades' eyes express the gravity of the circumstances better than any living pupils. His widely separated words are strangely related to those empty holes. He tells himself that what has just taken place is the most serious, the most extraordinary event imaginable. Death has been struck to the very root, for the first time in a million years. If the breach is not closed, Death will never recover. And the whole edifice of the universe will fall apart.

He lends his ear to his various ministers, and their words are just as gloomy, if not more so, than his own. Then he gives the order: Make ready my chariot!

He rides his chariot across the earth and the heavens, flying on to Olympus, to meet Zeus, the god of gods.

No one was ever to know what went on up there between them, neither how Hades awoke from divine slumber he whom none dared disturb, nor what all the others on Olympus said, or shouted, or sighed. No one was ever to know the voices they took on to mask their identities, or even the way they pronounced words backwards so their enemies could not understand them. There were never any leaks.

Lights go on in the gods' villas and offices. Chariots dash through the night. Various classes of investigators are roused: special intelligence officers, then the spies who investigate special intelligence officers, then those who keep an eye on the spies. And in all the hustle and bustle the whole of the ministry's staff awakens — professional delators, epileptic whistle-blowers, informers whose words are believed once in a thousand years, lead-swinging supervisors, allegedly blind tipsters, people who claim they would prefer to die rather than cease to be informers, and, in their train, all the cloak-and-dagger men, along with the bisexual scouts, the decoders of posthumous messages, the intuitives, the lunatics, and dealers in every kind of hocus-pocus. Old files are reopened, men and gods put to torture, a great hole dug — who knows why! — in the middle of Mount Olympus, and a column dropped into it straight away. Other incomprehensible acts follow, some for the first time ever, others for the last, and yet others that would have happened anyway, or which appear to be happening right now.

It comes to a point where time, whose flow has been stopped, seems about to burst its banks. Some of the gods go mad, perch on roofs, wait for the disaster. As time has apparently ceased to exist, nobody can say how long the panic went on. Consequently, nobody will ever be able to say whether it was dawn or dusk when the cry went out: "We've caught the culprit!"

In chains, with eyes swollen from beatings, the prisoner is dragged right to the top of Olympus. Rubberneckers congregate to get a look, and all around they exclaim, "So it was Tantalus who did this monstrous thing?"

Everybody has their eyes on the Great Prison where, according to the rumor, Zeus in person is to conduct the interrogation of the guilty party. People try to anticipate the questions: How did you manage to steal that? Who helped you? How did you carry the booty back down to earth?

But now darkness descends once more. Nobody will ever

know the questions that were actually asked. And our ignorance does not stop there. Nobody will ever know what really happened, how the crime was solved, how things returned to normal thereafter.

When it wakes up again, Olympus seems all sleepy-eyed. After its indeterminate absence, dawn doesn't quite know how to come upon the world, having lost its old habits. Here and there you can still see a few puddles of night lying around, with garbage collectors trying to shovel it up as if it were night soil. The whole place is buzzing with rumors about immortality. Some people think of it as an infinite number of particles spread around the body; others imagine it as a device that can be redirected toward the impossible; but most people see it as a key to some secret door. But these ramblings do not last long. By noontime, the stories have become utterly muddled. . . . In the taverns, people say that Tantalus was less greedy for immortality than he was for food and drink. The crimes he committed — which still cannot be named — should be put down to his insatiable appetite. They even say he's going to be sent down to hell for voracity.

Days go by, but things don't calm down: they get harsher. The rumors decrease in number and variety, but that's because a poster denouncing all of them has been put up on walls. Hades' memoirs are banned; by the same order, his wife's newspaper is closed down for being too freethinking. Even uttering the pentasyllable *immortality* is now against the law. One of Zeus's advisers opines that in such circumstances it would be more appropriate not to ban use of the word but to empty it of all content. After some hesitations, this opinion prevails. Persons previously considered merely illustrious — poets, sculptors, war leaders, even great courtesans — will be designated henceforth as "immortals."

News of this new yardstick spreads in no time at all. It is a gift of the gods to the mortals on earth, and they are grateful. Each time the gods now skim through news from mortal humanity, they can barely control their anger and contempt. You really thought you'd become immortal, you little insects? But there are major reasons why they have to hide their resentment. Anything that helps keep the greatest mystery of the universe hidden has to be accepted. They may have the minds of gods, but their brains go cloudy when they try to fathom where Death's exit door might be found. There is no such way out, the older gods declare. So put the temptation to the side. Even after torture and endless cross-examinations, Tantalus himself never lets out anything comprehensible on that subject. Maybe he acted like a sleepwalker, under the influence of an alien idea that had come to him from some other world? An alien idea that had perhaps been lost along the way, an idea that landed here by chance, before taking fright and fleeing in search of its own home?

More than a hundred thousand years later — maybe two hundred or five hundred thousand years later — Mark Gurabardhi lay with his hands clasped in the nape of his neck, trying to figure out all these questions. Maybe they were like the questions that would soon be put to the robbers who had held up the National Bank — even if the crime of distant Olympus was unlike any other.

He could picture the sinister two-story police barracks, and his face twisted into a scowl. All the same, he knew what the questions would be when they got the holdup men inside: Did anyone give you information about access to the bank? What means did you use to force the safe? Did you know what was inside it? Where have you hidden the money . . . the jewels . . . the crumbs of immortality?

CHAPTER 3

SHE HAD HAD HER HAIR DONE differently once again, but the style she had chosen really didn't match the vaguely absent expression on her face. Any other time, she would have lit up the whole room with her smile, posing with her hips and arms like a runway model, and then teased him with a "Now, do you like me like this?"

But this time she didn't behave that way at all, as if she'd forgotten what she'd had done to her hair. As soon as she got into the studio she went over to the walls, inspecting them with what seemed to Mark a falsely interested eye, looking for the signs of the work that the locksmith had done.

"Are you having the doors reinforced as well?" she asked, with her back still turned.

Mark grunted "yes" in response. He was tempted to ask

what the matter was, but he feared that in touchy circumstances such as these, which often arose without any obvious cause, asking a question like that would only make things worse.

"You have a new hairdo?" he said at last. "It suits you very well."

"You think so? Thanks."

He brushed her cheek with his lips and could smell the perfume on her neck.

"They've just opened a modern hair salon," she said. "Have you seen it?"

He thought she looked a little pale in the face, as well as distracted, and the hollows above her cheekbones suggested she'd had a sleepless night. He gave her another cuddle. She didn't reject the overture, but she did nothing to encourage him either. As she lifted her arms to put them around his neck, Mark noticed the down that had begun to grow again under her armpits.

Mark realized with a glum foreboding that all her preening had just been for her stay in Tirana.

He slipped his hands down her back to her hips, and the feeling of her filmy underwear beneath the fabric of her dress made him bolder.

She stiffened and pushed him away. "No," she said, almost in a whisper.

No: that's how relations between a man and a woman begin to go cold, Mark thought.

"Is there anything wrong?" he inquired.

"No," she said again as she drew his hand away from her shoulder.

He could feel her awkwardness and stress.

"I don't understand," he protested grumpily. "If there's anything that's not right between us, then be frank and tell me."

She sighed deeply. "I don't know if I should . . . tell you."

Mark instantly regretted having spoken before thinking. He was also sorry he had pushed the discussion as if to the edge of a cliff. He was on the verge of shouting, I don't want to know! I am fed up enough as it is, but it was too late.

He guessed he knew what she had to tell him: I didn't want to bring it up, but since you insist, I won't hide anything. . . .

"As soon as you got back from your trip, I knew something had happened," he mumbled with his eyes turned away from her. "Up there, in Tirana, apparently."

"No, not in Tirana. Right here!"

Well, that takes the cake! Mark said to himself. The new hairstyle — he saw it now — was meant for the other man. . . . But to hell with it: every affair comes to an end! Such instantly invented self-consolation was hardly convincing.

"All the same, I think I have a right to know what this is about."

He was amazed to hear himself saying the exact opposite of what was actually in his mind. In truth, he would rather not ever know anything about it.

"Of course," she said. "However painful it may be, I'll try to explain. . . ."

Okay, go on and hit me! he thought. Cut me into little pieces!

He staggered, as if drunk, toward the low table and grasped a bottle of schnapps. Both the bottle and the glass into which he poured a shot were blotched with yellow and blue fingerprints. He offered her the glass, but as she declined with a shake of her head, he downed it himself, in one go.

She had begun to talk, but he didn't look at her. He kept on staring at the big windowpane as if, by averting his gaze, he could delay the emergence of the truth. And that is more or less what happened. Her words were virtually incomprehensible. She was talking about the gloomy atmosphere in her family home, as if a frost had begun to take hold of everything and was growing harsher by the day. You would have thought she was talking about the frost coming down from the high peaks as winter sets in. At one point, Mark gave a deep sigh, as if he'd begun to grasp at least something of what she was going on about. As he heard her talk about "the old ways," he first thought it was about an arranged marriage; in other words, that she had to get engaged — but she shook her head vigorously and quickly set him straight. No, no, it was something much more serious, and therefore, of course, much more sinister. Nonetheless, it was still all utterly confused. Even she couldn't figure it out, because things were apparently being kept from her.

But now her family was expecting the arrival of an aged uncle. . . .

He was on the verge of muttering, What's your old uncle have to do with all this? Which stone did he crawl out from under? Why are you all so anxious to see him? But she didn't give Mark time to grumble.

"You told me about the permanent stress of life under the dictatorship," she went on in the same tired voice. "Obviously, you can't say that things are the same today. Nonetheless, the atmosphere in my family right now is just as suffocating. . . ."

Irritated by this, Mark shook his head sharply.

"No!" he said, raising his voice. "No anguish or terror can ever equal that! Not ever!"

He was coming close to losing the cool that he had only just recovered after his bout of jealousy. His girlfriend's last remarks were like an insult — as if she doubted him, after all that he had told her about the Communist years.

He was about to yell out loud, So tell me what this is all about! What's behind this worry and stress? An incurable disease, a crime, a threat?

Her eyes suggested she had to make a great effort to find the right words.

"Have you heard about the revival of ancient traditions?" she asked after a moment's silence.

Mark gave a cautiously affirmative response — but as if to restrict his "ye . . . s" even more, he added that lots of things that had been in the news recently, especially stories filed by foreign journalists, seemed to him to be rather exaggerated.

"I used to think so, too," she said.

The painter poured himself another drink.

"Vendettas are back! The terrible law of the *Kanun* has been restored!" he bawled in a theatrical baritone, and then burst out laughing. "It's nonsense! Journalists' twaddle!"

"You really believe that?"

"Sure," said Mark. "Don't you?"

The young woman smiled a faint but bitter smile.

"I don't know what to say," she began, unsteadily. "Everything is so dark. . . ."

Abruptly and for no clear reason, but maybe because the sorrow he could see in her eyes struck him as quite different, almost alien, he regretted having let himself get carried away. He stroked her hair gently and asked:

"Is there . . . something like that going on . . . at home?"

He had to ask her twice before she felt entitled to speak about it. She was still not making very much sense. Yes, of course, there was something of that sort going on at home. Her brother Angelin had been in a kind of daze for almost a week. But nobody would tell her anything. She wondered if they were waiting for the uncle from Shala Province to come and explain it all to her.

"But just who is this uncle?" Mark broke in. "I meant to ask you already: why the hell are you all waiting for this uncle?"

"What do you mean, why? He's the one who's going to explain it all!"

"Oh, I see now. He's going to decide if you — if your family is or is not tangled up in one of these old stories. Wait a minute, the old saying is coming back to me: If your family has anything to do with a blood feud . . ."

From this point on, Mark thought he understood why their conversation had been so awkward. The very language they now spoke was no longer appropriate to the subject matter. They would have had to go back to the old language, whose source had gone dry long ago, like a water pipe all clogged with lime.

There was a long silence. Once again, Mark thought he heard something banging against the windowpane. But if it was a knock, it was clearly intended for someone else.

"A vendetta coming back to life after lying dormant for fifty years . . . Frankly, I can't take that seriously!" Mark declared.

He sounded quite sincere, and, as a matter of fact, he really did not believe it was possible. It was probably the *Kanun*'s last spasm, its dying effort to come up to the surface, along with everything else that had been pushed down to the bottom by the prohibitions of the Communist era. Mark wasn't saying this just to reassure his girlfriend. At the turn of the millennium, the *Kanun* had outlived its natural life span. It would have died a natural death long ago had it not been banned by the Communists. Their attempt to suppress it was the only reason this madness had acquired new life.

She listened to him with wide eyes in which tears seemed to be on the point of welling up.

"My dearest darling," he said to her tenderly as he kissed her hair, thinking all the while, My Beatrice. . . .

The woman he had wanted to have as his guide to the new era now turned out to be held back by an ancient and rusty hook.

She calmed down and started explaining again what was going on in her home. She used the word "cold" so often that Mark imagined she was actually shivering. He poured out another glass of schnapps, and this time she agreed to drink her round. As he put his hand on her knees, then between her legs, her speech slowed, and gave way to little gasps. This time, she sighed, instead of groaning in her usual way; but maybe Mark only thought this because her final outburst was a sound he had never heard before, an alien sound that seemed to come from the throat of a different person.

As he lay motionless beside her, he realized that anyone listening attentively in the offices downstairs might have thought that he had not been making love to his girlfriend, but strangling her to death.

She left the studio, and Mark went out shortly after, but before going back to his office, he put in an appearance at the café. All the dailies were strewn about the tables, as always, but Mark didn't have the patience to skim through them.

"Anything up?" he asked the waiter when the latter brought him his coffee.

"Not a thing. The new police chief was supposed to lay his hands on the bank robbers by the end of the week, but he's not done a thing so far. Apparently his hands are not as free as he would like. He grumbles about not getting any help at all."

"Really? None at all?"

"The rest of the news is the usual gossip and nonsense. They're claiming that before dawn this morning the leader of the opposition sent a fax to some lady in the Council of Europe — and the fax was nine yards long! How about that, eh? Nine yards of fax, and at five in the morning! In a pinch, you could call that sexual harassment!"

Mark chuckled.

"And all these blood feud killings they keep going on about — are they true, or just space fillers cooked up by journalists short of real news?"

The waiter pursed his lips. "Hmm . . . That depends on how you look at it. One of my cousins came down from Hoti and told me that they'd had cases of that kind up there these last few weeks. But —"

"But what?"

"Well, God only knows if it really is a blood feud, like in the old days, or something quite different. . . . Things are in such a muddle at the moment!"

"And are there really any people who've shut themselves up at home, who've cloistered themselves in their *kulla*, like they used to?"

"I've heard tell of some. But you know as well as I do that people like to embroider. . . . Some poor fellow stays at home because he's got backache, and the next thing you know, people are saying he's been cloistered as part of a blood feud!"

They both laughed.

"I find it all rather strange," the waiter went on. "It's as if it was just a game. But if they really do unearth the *Book of the Blood* — and you do hear people talking about it — then it'll be quite a different kettle of fish, believe you me."

"The *Book of the Blood*? Yeah, I think I heard of something of that sort."

Any other time the waiter would have been dumbfounded by such ignorance, but Mark, even though he had been living in B—— for some years, was still considered a newcomer to the North.

"Well, as you've no doubt heard, this book is a list of all blood feuds since the beginning," the waiter explained. "Who redeemed the blood, and who still has to do some redeeming, who still has a blood debt and who hasn't; it even lays down cases where there is just a half-blood still to pay off. . . . In other words, when that book comes to light, we'd all better keep inside four walls. If it does come to light, that is . . ."

"And where exactly do they expect to lay their hands on it?" Mark queried.

"Nobody knows where it is. They've looked high and low, so they say. They've been down into the secret section of the National Archives more than once, according to gossip. But in fact nobody even knows where the Secret Archives really are. Some say they are in deep storage right here, up in these mountains. I must confess I don't really believe that. People are saying the same thing in at least three different parts of Albania."

When Mark came out of the café, he felt as if he'd just taken a sleeping pill. Some days he rather liked that sluggish torpor. At the crossroads, he slowed his pace to read the obituary notices posted on the wall. He read them slowly, line by line, as if he was deciphering difficult old texts. Then he shook his head, almost in fright. God knows why, but he felt as if he had just been looking for the name of his old friend Zef.

It was hustle and bustle at the Arts Center. A computer was being installed in the director's office. In a week's time — two weeks at the most — a delegation from the Council of Europe was due to visit. Still no news about the holdup at the bank. The music section was having a coffee break, as usual.

Mark lit a cigarette and slumped into one of his armchairs. Before opening his mouth to say anything about the *Book of the Blood,* he speculated on the reactions his question was likely to provoke. Someone might go pale, another might look dumbstruck, and yet another tell him to shut up. All the same, he would go right ahead.

The subject didn't leave his mind all week long. At one point he wondered if he was not already obsessed with it; but then he told himself it was quite natural for it to be going around and around in his head, seeing that his girlfriend was directly involved. But did he really want the *Book of the Blood* to be found? At times, he reckoned that bringing it to light would prompt the much-desired miracle: your family has been worrying about nothing, you've no blood debt to pay, nor any to collect. . . .

When he told this to his girlfriend, she shook her head in doubt. The memory of the old was quite as reliable as the book. If the old uncle were to state that the family was entangled in a blood feud, that would be as good as holy writ. He would already have been there actually, if he hadn't had another attack of gout. But he had let them know that he would come, even if he had to be carried down on a stretcher.

May his legs drop off! Mark thought to himself. He grinned inwardly at his own thought, for it was the first time that he had caught himself uttering curses like a man of old.

What was known of the fate of the *Book of the Blood* up until World War II was generally consistent; but what had happened to it thereafter was the subject of widely divergent stories. When they came to power in 1945, the Communists burned down the Castle of Orosh, where the book had been kept for many centuries. At first it was supposed that the book had turned to ashes along with a part of the archives of the prince of Orosh, but soon after a different supposition came into circulation, namely, that the *Book of the Blood* had been stashed away safely somewhere else. That seemed all the more plausible when the suspicion that the Communists had gotten hold of it and destroyed it themselves turned out to be unjustified. After all, if the winning side had gone so far as to preserve the historical records of land ownership, it was hardly likely that it would have suppressed a mortal inventory. The *Book of the Blood* had rightly been called a "Domesday Book of Death" by a journalist of that period. For the Communists, property was a threat far greater than death!

One after another, people who still whispered about it came around to the view that the book still existed, in some secret hiding place. What no one knew was who had secreted it. Some thought that opponents of the new regime had hidden it safely — like the holy relics from the Church of Saint Anthony, the original emblem of the Dugagjin clan, an eleventh-century portrait of the Virgin, and various other treasures which it was obviously desirable to save from destruction. But there were others who thought that the book had been hidden by the Communists themselves. Having decided to put an end to the thousand-year-old system of customary law called the *Kanun*, they must have decided they needed to begin with its accounting system, the *Book of the Blood*. Some people of this persuasion went even further and speculated that the secret agents of the Sigurimi had started to use the book for their own sinister purposes. On reflection, though, that would have been only natural.

In later years, a cloak of silence fell on the *Kanun*, and the book sank into oblivion. Even the muffled rumors that could still be heard now and again seemed barely related to the original speculations, and they were far less sensational. In many cases, the rumors seemed to be only reflections of some public event. For example, when Maurice Thorez, the leader of the French Communist Party, visited Albania, people claimed he had been presented with a silver pistol — and the *Book of the Blood*. The same story was told about Nikita Khrushchev, the Soviet leader, and then again, some years later, about Franz-Josef Strauss, when, oddly enough, Albania was trying to improve relations with West Germany. Some people, it seemed, were absolutely determined to believe that Albania would pass the fearful book on to another nation.

When the dictatorship fell, many books about the *Kanun* were published, and there was renewed talk of the notorious ledger. The old speculations about its fate were put back into circulation, together with new guesses, some of which were quite crazy, as was the press in general at that time. In the Book it will all be found! some journalist wrote: our trial, and our judgment! Another journalist riposted, You'd better go and get hold of your personal file, you wretch, if you want to know what particular sentence you are under! In Tirana, there were as many gradations in rumors about the Book as in a musical scale. In one variant, the book was said to have been requested by the Helsinki Committee; in another, it was not the OSCE, but the International Court at The Hague that had requisitioned it. "And why, dear sir, should the International Court of Justice have subpoenaed our book?" "How should I know?" came the reply. "Maybe we're under suspicion of genocide? It's a very fashionable expression these days!" "Genocide of whom? By whom?" "Oh, stop getting on my nerves. Why should I know by whom and to whom? Maybe by the Albanians . . . against the Albanians?" "Aha, so that's what the score is, then!"

Well, that was the kind of argument you could hear in the cafés of the capital. But in the little town of B——, it all had a very different impact.

The afternoon suddenly seemed to have gone dead, as if it had been abandoned: a not uncommon impression toward the end of August, foreshadowing the coming autumn. A singer could be heard far away, and the monotonous strain only heightened the feeling of emptiness.

Mark looked at his watch. The locksmith should have finished installing his new front door by now. He dressed, went out, and made for his studio.

The streets were deserted. The singer's voice grew nearer. Mark could now make out the words:

I'm waiting for you in Station Road
Stand up straight, pretty girl, stand up straight!

Good Lord, what a stupid ditty! Mark thought. He had to listen for a while to make out the rest of it:

The boy is dying of love
Stand up straight, pretty girl, stand up straight!

It would have been hard to find a tune better fitted to this desolate provincial Sunday afternoon. Mark hurried on so as not to hear the song, but just as the unknown singer had faded into the distance, Mark found himself repeating the refrain:

Stand up straight, pretty girl, stand up straight!

It occurred to him that that was precisely how provincial dull-wittedness spreads from person to person. But that didn't stop him from inwardly regurgitating those pointless words, in spite of himself, all the way back to the studio.

The locksmith had indeed finished the job. He had even stuck up a piece of paper next to the new door with the warning "Take Care! Wet Paint!"

Mark took his new key from his pocket, opened his new door, and then walked around his studio as if checking that nothing else had been changed inside it. The craftsman had told him that anyone, but especially an artist, feels different once he has an armored door.

He stopped for a moment in front of his unfinished nude, then, as his eye wandered toward the El Greco copy, his mind returned once again to the image of Philip II sinking slowly toward death at the Escorial. Like any king, he, too, must have wondered how best to make his doors protect him from intrusion.

To his considerable surprise, however, Mark did not feel safer; quite the opposite. In any case, he was ready to drop. The fitting of the new door had only made him tired. He lay down, back to the bay window, to shade his eyes from the light. Evening was coming on quite fast. It was a strange kind of dusk, for unlike an ordinary sundown, the heavenly orb was still shining at full strength. . . . At first he barely heard the knocking on the door, but soon the noise made by the messengers of Death grew ever more perceptible. Mark reached around himself with fevered movements to find the talisman of immortality, but he just could not remember where he had put it away. The hammering on the other side of the door got more and more violent. Only when Mark shouted "Enough!" did silence return.

It was the shout that woke him up. He looked at the bay window, then at the door. All his thinking about the door must have set off the nightmare, he decided.

"You won't be getting any visitors now!" the locksmith had told him. "Your art's quite safe till kingdom come."

Mark smiled to himself without bothering to explain out loud that he'd heard "your heart's quite safe"; that is, he had become more or less immortal. The cards had gotten shuffled in his poor head: immortals get burgled, whereas mediocre and mortal folk never have their things stolen. . . .

His eyes alighted once again on the bay window. The watery light of the dying day was slowly fading away in a kind of haughty despair. He stood up and paced the studio floor once again.

Night had fallen when he went out. Before going to have dinner at the restaurant, he wandered past the block where Zef lived. The windows of his third-floor apartment were still dark.

"Where are you, Zef?" he cried out silently.

He continued on, trying to think of nothing at all. What peace! he said to himself as he stopped to light a cigarette. Was that a distant lowing he could hear? He went on his way, but stopped again immediately, since the distant noise sounded out a second time. It couldn't be confused with the howling of the wind or with an echo from the mountain valleys. It was a rumbling that seemed to arise from an unimaginable depth and an impossible distance. Like the unending aftershock of the big bang rolling on eternally throughout the universe. And maybe that's what it really is! Mark decided.

CHAPTER 4

IT TOOK NO MORE THAN A COUPLE of customers talking loudly at one of the five tables of the Town Café to make it seem like there was something going on. That morning, there was heated conversation at two of the said tables, and at both of them the discussion was so lively that a stranger coming into the room and wanting to get into the thick of things would have had a hard time deciding which table to sit at.

Mark hesitated himself as he stood in the door, but not for the same reason. When he could see that neither table was likely to calm down, he went up to the bar and stood alongside Cuf Kertolla, sitting by himself, as usual, with a glass in front of him. They can say what they like! thought Mark. He knew that the bar crowd took him for a standoffish and unsociable fellow, a stuck-up from the capital, or even a has-been, but he didn't give a damn.

"They've got problems," Cuf muttered as he nodded toward the noisy customers at the tables.

Mark pretended not to have heard and ordered a coffee. But however hard you tried to keep out of it, you couldn't help picking up the main topic of conversation. At one of the tables, they were debating whether the new head of state was more afraid of his predecessor, the man whose place he had taken, than that predecessor had been of the terrifying leader he had replaced and who was, thank God, no longer of this world. At the other table, the drinkers were talking of some Judas or other who was expected to arrive from the capital, or who had maybe already arrived in discreet disguise. He was supposed to have denounced some prominent writers back in Tirana, and God only knew why he was now traipsing around in the provinces.

"They've really got problems!" Cuf Kertolla said again, but speaking directly to Mark this time. "They talk big, these Albanians! Always going on about heads of state, the UN, or Bible stories. But they don't mention the holes in their own underpants! Say, do you know if they're going to make us pay taxes?"

Cuf showed how proud he was of the relevance of his question by raising his eyebrows.

"No, I have no idea," Mark answered.

"Apparently, we Albanians, after having suffered from all

kinds of divisions and splits — Communists and bour-
geois, northerners and southerners, Catholics and Muslims,
and the devil knows how many other factions — we Albanians, I was saying, are giving it all up so as to form two new
grand parties: the Talls and the Smalls. Have you already
heard about that?"

"No," said Mark, "I haven't."

"Well, it's like I said. The leader of the Talls is the king, of
course; he's nearly seven feet. As for the Smalls, they're under the whip of a fat little man from the South. It's going to
be a hoot!"

This time Mark said nothing. He drained his cup, paid,
and left.

Outside he could feel the first whiff of autumn weather.
The trees had already lost some of their leaves, and they
looked foreign and menacing. Most of them seemed to have
been designed as gallows, in any case.

Mark frowned and shook his head, as he did every time
he wanted to get a disagreeable thought out of his head. Listening to a conversation about Judas first thing in the morning was not the best way to put him in a good mood.

As he drew close to the City Arts Center, he heard the
sound of running right behind him. He turned around and
saw the head of the music section coming up.

"I went to look for you at the studio," he said, panting for
breath. "The boss sent me to get you. We're expecting a delegation this afternoon."

"Really? I'd just stopped to have a coffee." Mark laughed. "Have you heard of the two new parties — the Talls and the Smalls?"

"No," the musician replied. "But that wouldn't be so surprising."

"There are reports of an old spy turning up here, too. They even came up with his name, Judas, which did surprise me a bit. I didn't think anyone in this backwater would know any names."

"You know, I've stopped being surprised by the gossip that goes around. Yesterday, my father-in-law, whom I took to be a man of sense, tried to persuade me that the bank heist was masterminded by the opposition!"

They both laughed out loud at this. Since Zef had disappeared, Mark found that he enjoyed the company of the head of the music section more and more.

"So now Judas is going to get his teeth into us at last!" he said. "That's all that B—— has been waiting for!"

The City Arts Center was abuzz. The director's sky blue tie quivered with excitement, and his whole being exuded an air of euphoria.

"Is the delegation from Spain?" Mark inquired in an undertone.

"Mmm . . . up to a point, perhaps. The people are actually from the Council of Europe," the secretary explained. "But some of them might be from Spain."

The director went over their marching orders. The delegation would arrive around 3:00 P.M. So everyone was to be at their posts by 2:30. As for the other rules of engagement, staff members already knew them.

The foreigners showed up at 3:00 P.M. precisely. There were two Germans, one Dutchman, and an Albanian guide. First they had coffee at the Arts Center, then they asked to see the surrounding area. They wanted to visit a convent that had been reopened after being left to its own devices for the fifty years of Communist rule, and a *kulla,* or Tower of Refuge, of the highland folk.

The director climbed into the foreigners' car; Mark, with the head of the music section, got into the next, an aged Russian-made all-terrain vehicle originally leased to the ministry of the interior and then handed to the Arts Center after the fall of the old regime.

The bush-lined dirt road climbed on and on up into the mountains. There were not many towers, but they stopped at each one that came into sight. The Albanian guide — a tall lad with a sloping right shoulder beneath his check jacket — gave a commentary in German. The Accursed Mountains could just be made out on the far horizon. The cold air made the Germans' straw-colored hair look even thinner. The head of the music section, who stayed with Mark at the back of the party, twisted his head this way and that as if looking for something he had lost.

Mark thought he could hear a wolf howling in the distance, but no one else seemed to worry about it. It must have been the wind in the hills. He tried to imagine which steep path his girlfriend's fearsome uncle would take when he came down from the northern plateau.

"Listen, Mark," said the musician. "I don't know why, but I've got a strong feeling that the path to the storage depot of the Secret Archives is somewhere around here."

"Do you think so?" said Mark. "I've heard people say that sort of thing, but I thought it was just gossip."

"Well, no, it's not just another tall tale. It's true they could have been moved since then, but in 1985, when Hoxha died, the archives really were in these parts."

The area was undoubtedly suited to the role. A remote little spot at the foot of the Accursed Mountains: you couldn't have dreamed of a more inaccessible hole.

"The cave must be somewhere nearby, I swear," the music section head went on. "One of my cousins who worked for the Interior told me a very odd story about that." He slowed his pace so as not to catch up with the main party. Mark was staring hard at him. "In April 1985, three days after the death of the tyrant, the first thing his successor did, just as soon as he had been sworn in, was to make a secret visit to B——."

"No kidding?"

"It's what my cousin told me at the time. It was the most discreet flying visit ever. Just two cars, so as not to attract attention."

"That's very odd," Mark mumbled.

"Well, the next part is even odder," the musician added. Although they were now way behind the visiting foreigners, they slowed their pace even more. "The small delegation from Tirana arrived precisely at 10:00 P.M. They didn't stop in town and went straight to the deep storage depot. And there" — the head of the music section was already speaking in a whisper, but now, so it seemed to Mark, he was almost singing a lullaby — "and there, the new head of state hunted for things until three in the morning."

"Well, well," said Mark. "And then what?"

"Aren't you going to ask me what he was looking for?" Mark shrugged. "Well, that is the question! What was he really after? I've puzzled over that so many times since then! No one has the faintest idea. Nor does anyone know if he found what he was looking for. My cousin was one of the small group of local officials who escorted the head of state to the cave, and he said that when the leader came out, he looked utterly depressed."

The director was shouting from way up front: "Hey, you two! Get a move on, we're on our way!"

He sounded just a little resentful of their confabulating out of earshot, but both of them knew that the boss was so delighted to be mingling with foreigners, they could bend the rules a little without making him angry.

"We were talking about the *Kanun*," the head of the music section said as he and Mark rejoined the main group.

"Really?" The director's face clouded over. "That's all people are interested in these days!" he said with a kind of sadness, and turned his back on them.

It was known in B—— that the director felt let down

when visitors expressed interest in the old traditions. He was anxious to get down to talking about the latest advances of human civilization, about the Internet, the common currency, anything that had to do with the future of Europe. But to his amazement, foreigners not only spoke of such things without the least passion, but also couldn't wait to quiz him about the old *Kanun*. How do you account for its revival? Do Towers of Refuge still exist? Were the ancient rules going to come back in a big way?

The two cars stopped in front of the convent. The foreigners snapped photographs of the restored gateway and walls. Once again, Mark thought he could hear that wolf in the distance. Images of his girlfriend's armpits, of her uncle's damaged leg, and of his much-allayed suspicion of her having had an affair in Tirana whirled about in his head.

The road ahead of them was virtually impassable, and the director reminded everyone that they had to be back in town before nightfall. Mark happened to notice the Albanian guide and interpreter just as he was bending down to get back in the car, and it suddenly occurred to him that what the Judas people were gossiping about was perhaps none other than he. The check jacket he was wearing somehow seemed to confirm the suspicion. God knows why, but he had always imagined that spies wore clothes of that sort.

On the way back, the cars passed by the hillside where the tunnel leading to the Secret Archives was supposed to be located. With his face pressed hard against the side window, Mark's eyes hunted for some trace of an opening, but his breath misted up the glass. What had the head of state come to look for down in that hole? A message, a secret register, maybe his own file, kept there in case they might have to blackmail him, too? The dictator, people said, used that kind of armlock more and more as he grew old, to keep members of the Politburo totally dependent on him. So if it had seemed convenient to keep killer files on the others, it must have been even more necessary to keep information of last resort on the man who was to be his successor.

Mark had a feeling the head of the music section was having similar thoughts. He said to him in a whisper, "I can't get what you told me about the deep storage of state secrets out of my head."

"I'm not surprised. After my cousin first told me about it, the mystery obsessed me for weeks."

Obviously it would have, Mark thought. It raised a question of no small importance. What could the new Great Guide have been looking for in the dark, with a flashlight, the very moment he gained supreme power? What crime, what stain, did he have on his conscience?

All that spring and right through to the following winter, people never ceased to wonder whether the new president had murdered anyone. His supporters compared him — so as to whitewash him, if only a little — to the dead dictator and all the terror and horrors his reign had brought. The skeptics would not abandon their position that no one could have climbed so high without many a foul deed on his way up.

Mark was one of the skeptics. As Gentian used to say, crime is one of the most remarkable jewels in the crown of Communist potentates. Without it, the crown would be as precious as papier-mâché.

The two cars, traveling together, were now approaching the town. The first streaks of dusk in the sky made it look as if it was going to snow up in the hills.

Mark was exhausted. Words that sounded like the lyrics of a forgotten tune rang around his head:

Up in the mountain lies my fine secret . . .

Yes, it was like a snippet of an old folktale, of the kind you can never remember having read or heard for the first time: Once upon a time, there was a new ruler who lived in a palace in the capital. But his secret power, his soul, his very essence, was shut up in a casket buried deep beneath one of these great hills. . . .

Mark and the head of music went to look for the hall where the meeting was scheduled to take place. An acquaintance told him on the telephone that it was in a warehouse that had been used for a while as an adult movie house. Nowadays, the owner rented it out for meetings, most often to religious sects and political factions.

"Renaming the streets, that's another part of the muddle!" the head of music said to him. "Each time the town elects a different party, the first thing the new councillors do is change the street names. Right-wingers abolish names like 'The Three Martyrs' and put back the ancient sign invoking 'Our Immaculate Lady,' and the leftists, when they get back in power, do just the same, only in reverse."

Erotic graffiti on the walls indicated they were on the right track. They could see the half-opened metal doors of the warehouse from quite a distance.

"Isn't this going to be dangerous?" Mark asked. "I mean, should we have invitations to be allowed in?"

"No, no, not at all," said his friend.

They tried to make themselves as unremarkable as they could as they filed into the long, bare hall. At the back, sitting behind a table decked with a scarlet rug, were two men: an old man in highland folk dress, and another, pale-faced and smooth-skinned, wearing a felt hat. He must have been on edge, but his unwrinkled skin was probably the reason why his irritation could not be read on his face. Despite that, anger was in the air: you could see it in the trembling tassels of the scarlet tablecloth.

"We are all well aware that the *Kanun* has changed for the worse. What we need is to rid it of the filth and madness that is strangling it to death nowadays. That's what we're here to discuss. With as little bullshit as we can manage."

Someone sitting in the middle of the hall shouted out, "The Russian Kalashnikov, that's the *Kanun*'s number-one enemy!"

A great roar of applause and booing broke out instantly in the hall.

"You, sir, stand up and spell out your reasons!" said the platform speaker in the felt hat.

So the man stood up.

Everyone in the hall turned to look at him, so Mark could see the faces of all the participants. They had turned their heads with such lack of ease that Mark almost expected to hear their necks creak like rusty hinges. He shuddered. In those frozen faces that looked as though they had been rescued from the morgue, the only trace of life was in the eyes. They glowed like embers in the wind. But there were other faces in the assembly to which the opposite had happened: faces where the eyes seemed to have gone dead first.

"The Kalashnikov rifle, like everything that comes from the Slav, undermines the *Kanun*," the speaker explained. "We learned from our forebears, as they learned from theirs, that the *Kanun* is about one shot — the first shot. When you've pulled the trigger, you've had your due. It's now your opponent's turn to shoot at you. A second shot is not allowed by the *Kanun*, and a third shot even less, so the thirty-odd bullets that come out of a Kalashnikov belt have nothing at all to do with the rules. But that's what people are using these days to apply the old laws! It's shameful!"

Several men approved with a "Well said!" or a "Right you are!"

The speaker now got into his stride.

"The *Kanun* does not allow the use of knives, axes, fire,

or stone. Nor does it condone drowning, strangling, whipping, or the use of explosives."

"That's absolutely correct!" men shouted out around the hall.

"Well, then, why are people doing all these things nowadays? These are shameful practices, and they must be stopped!"

The crowd of men expressed approval by rapping their knuckles on the seat backs in front of them.

"Where do these folk come from? How did they know about the meeting tonight?" Mark whispered into the ear of his friend.

"God only knows."

On the way to the hall, the musician had explained to Mark that, according to what he had picked up, such assemblies — which had the appearance of political meetings, which were now quite legal — used to be held when there was a perceived need to amend an article or clause of the old Code of Laws of the *Kanun*. But they had always been very infrequent, happening maybe once every hundred or two hundred years.

Mark's lungs felt close to bursting. It was a special kind of anxiety that he felt each time he was present at some exceptional event without fully appreciating just what he was witnessing. This meeting had the power to arouse emotions appropriate to events that happen only once in a lifetime. The huge gaps of time between each of these assemblies and the next — whole generations could pass through this world without ever having heard of them — made this night all the more daunting. It must have been at a general assembly of this kind in the distant past that the huge decision to replace knives with guns had once been taken.

Another man had risen to speak. He was demanding that a proclamation be drawn up and read out in every village by criers, just like in the old days.

The last speaker observed that after fifty years in deep freeze, the *Kanun*, unlike other corpses that are kept intact by ice and snow, had emerged in a sorry state. For the time being, it was everyone's duty to speak out against the distortions of the old Code, and to call a halt to any further degradation. This speech prompted more knuckle-rapping on the seat backs.

Suddenly Mark thought he had caught sight of Zef. Yes, that was the nape of his neck, and the cheekbone was just like his; but the man kept his head stock-still. No, it can't be, Mark thought, I must be hallucinating.

He felt a buzzing in his forehead and a weight against his temple that made his mind go cloudy, as it did every time that he thought of Zef.

Who knows what had become of Zef since they last met? Had he changed? A set of mental slides passed in front of his eyes: Zef as a factory boss whose workers had only ever seen his signature; Zef on a rubber dinghy, smuggling passengers across the Strait of Otranto; Zef lying in silk sheets with a naked woman; Zef lying at the bottom of the sea. . . .

The noise of people striking the seat backs with their

hands brought him back to himself. His friend muttered something in his ear. The assembly seemed to be going on forever.

In the end, they both got out of their seats and made their exit as discreetly as they had come. Dusk was falling. It seemed to Mark that the folk in the hall had deliberately stuck to saying the obvious on purpose, since hard thinking would have required too much effort.

Mark and his friend parted company at the first crossroads. On his way back to the studio, Mark went down Friars Street. As usual, there was no light in the windows of Zef's third-floor apartment.

He lit a cigarette and tried to blank out everything from his mind.

The studio door made a creaking noise as he opened it. It would go on creaking like that until it had properly settled on its hinges, the locksmith had said. But there was a piece of paper, folded twice over, under the door. He bent down, picked it up, and as he read it he realized with alarm that the handwriting was his girlfriend's:

"My uncle got here today. Nothing is quite sorted out yet. *Je t'embrasse.*"

He stood quite still for a moment with the letter in his hand. So the highland uncle had turned up. Judas too, he thought despondently.

The trumpets were sounding.

By Way of a Counter-Chapter. Fever

THE VIRUSES WERE SPREADING ALL OVER. Most of them had no names. You thought you had a cold and ended up having tests for leprosy.

Mark had a fever. At times he felt as if he was turning endless somersaults down to the deepest basement in the universe. He was going down and down, in an elevator falling faster and faster, at vertiginous speed, toward Dante's Inferno. The abrupt rediscovery of things that had been buried deep since time immemorial was something he could not stand. The old secrets were like oil fields without any soul or remorse, like sorrowful seams of long-abandoned coal, or a lode of sapphire giving off occasional smiling cynical sparkles. . . .

When he came out of this whirlpool, he found himself in stark silence, beneath still waters, and that was just as unbearable. Nothing stirred; there was not the slightest breath of movement in the reed bed over there. All passion was spent, not a spark of human excitement was permitted. It was just a specimen book filled with dried Furies mounted like butterflies and identified at the bottom of each page by an inventory number and a Latin botanical name.

One afternoon Mark's fever dropped a little. He realized he was not so sick when it occurred to him, without the slightest hesitation or doubt, that he knew who the real bank robbers were. At least, he knew who two of them were: Palok Kuqi and Cuf Kertolla, the man who propped up the bar at the Town Café. Things often turn out like that — you hunt high and low for clues, but the culprits have been in front of you all along, even sipping a cup of coffee right next to you. Mark felt too weary to work out how he had come by his certain knowledge. But next to the horror of falling and the terror he had felt, this seemed perfectly natural.

Then his fever went up again. No! no! he moaned intermittently. He was being pestered by the iceberg that sank the *Titanic*, which insisted on his hearing its confession. You're the assistant commissioner, the iceberg said, so you have to take my confession! I really must lay down my burden of remorse! But nobody's blaming you! Mark pointed out, but he didn't dare speak the truth, that nobody in the force wanted to waste time on a lump of ice. Notwithstanding, the iceberg had already begun to pour out the story of its so-called life. It had been born when the *Titanic* was no more than a set of lines and numbers on a naval architect's drawing boards. One winter's night, its parents, two giant North Sea icebergs, collided, and from that amorous encounter, or monstrous crash, as you will, the young one was born. Like any newborn babe he was quite small at the start, but he grew and grew in height and weight. It was very cold, and as everyone knows there's nothing better for the health than living on cold and nothing else. I was the son of the frost, and the frost was my master. Other people, like you, say that cold is death, but for us, it's the opposite, it's heat that is death. That's the great gulf of misunderstanding that keeps us apart. And that's where the famous accident of the night of April 14 comes from. I, the antisun, was solitary and cold, and found myself staring at the brand-new *Titanic*. But you can't understand that. Your god is warmth. In your lust for heat you're capable of anything, you could even burn the world down. See now: a few minutes ago you were complaining of being cold, and now your forehead is burning and all you dream of is an ice cube to put on it!

That's true enough, Mark said to himself. But he did not quite know how to apologize. The fact that the huge ship *Titanic*, with its deck lights and searchlights, with its roaring boilers and its cabin fires, with its freight of smiles, music, and champagne, with its women's unshaven love nests, should have smashed into the guardian of the glacial realm now seemed to Mark to be the most natural thing in the world.

Two entities made of opposite elements had come up

against each other in the wrong place, somewhere they should never have been together, just like that other case, that other story. . . . That's right, in that faraway town where a man and a snake, like people who have to share a single suit of clothes, had shared the same physical appearance.

Mark wanted to yell: Not now! Some other time, please! But he knew it would have been a waste of breath. The snake was another one who wanted charges brought. He told the whole story in the generally accepted version, in other words toeing what could be called the official line. Before quizzing him on the other, secret version, Mark wanted to know more about the moment of transition, the moment that seemed to be not of this world, the instantaneous flash in which the metamorphosis of man into reptile and reptile into man took place. That's the sole matter on which I would be grateful not to answer any questions, the snake replied. It cannot be told. Even if I wanted to tell you about it, I could not. You said it yourself: It's not of this world; as a consequence, any attempt to understand it would fail, first of all, but would also quite possibly be a mortal sin.

I guess that's true, Mark thought.

As for the other, secret version, it was just the official story turned on its head, as it often is in so many cases: instead of the snake-groom turning into a man every night, it was the man-groom who could suddenly change into a snake. It was reminiscent of the story of an Albanian girl who had landed in Italy in 1999 after crossing the Strait of Otranto. In a hotel room in Bari, her boyfriend had sud-

denly turned into a wild animal. . . . A high proportion of
the Albanian prostitutes in Rome and Paris had more or less
the same story to tell. On each and every one of their wedding nights, the bridegroom had thrown off his human disguise, metamorphosed into an unrecognizable, alien being,
and insisted that his bride go work on the streets.

"How come there are now so many of you?" Mark asked,
but no answer came, as the snake had vanished.

As it's often been stated, all that happened at the time of
the gods' first departure. At the time, of course, nobody noticed at all. So we have lost the date of their departure and
the real reason for it; yet it must have become pretty obvious to all. Now the opposite rumor was doing the rounds:
the gods were coming back! They were returning from long
years of wandering, and only they knew how to come back.
(Maybe they were hitching rides in OSCE cars, or were using vehicles that mere mortals had not yet dreamed of.)
Come as you can, bring what you will, but don't leave us
alone! Mark screamed — and this time, he screamed it all
out loud.

He was hanging on to the tassels of his bedspread as if to
stop himself from falling into the pit.

CHAPTER 5

MARK WENT UP TO THE WINDOW to see what was going on outside. It was a most curious spectacle. The city was under water. Muddy brown water, the sort you see when there's been flooding. Even from the balcony you could hear the lapping of the waves. Mark leaned over, dipped his fingers in it, and was surprised to find that it was not at all cold. He was alarmed to see how rapidly the flood had risen to the level of his second-floor apartment, and for a short while he stared at the buildings on the other side of the street and at the tops of the lampposts, which rose above the waterline. Then without a second thought he stripped off his shirt, and, as he was already in his underpants, put his leg over the balustrade. He dipped a toe into the water, and then let the rest of him slip in.

For a short moment he wondered if he was dreaming; the quietness all around would otherwise have been inexplicable. But he soon realized that he was not in a dream. Everyone else seemed to be still asleep, unaware of what had happened during the night. In any case, it was very pleasant to swim about at second-floor level. Distances seemed somehow altered, crossroads seemed closer to each other, and Mark imagined he would get to his girlfriend's window very easily indeed. How surprised she would be to see him swim up to her bay window! He would hang on to the railing for a few seconds to get his breath back, and then haul himself up over it.

In the distance a siren — from a police car or some other emergency vehicle — could be heard blaring faintly. You're taking your time! Mark thought.

He swam toward the main crossroads at the center of town; with a bit more effort he could get to the town hall plaza and, farther on, to the Arts Center. On both sides of the street all sorts of things were stacked on people's balconies: sofas, bicycle wheels, and multicolored beach balls, which brought back to mind the summer holidays.

He suddenly thought of his studio, and shuddered with fear. What a muddlehead you are! he scolded himself. That's what you should have worried about first! He made a sharp about-turn, in order to swim back toward the studio. Some alleys were completely submerged, so he was able to take short cuts straight over the roofs of low shacks that he could barely see through the murky water.

His limbs, which up to then had moved with ease, now began to feel heavy. A panic came upon him. You must be crazy! he told himself a second time, as he craned his neck left and right to see if he really was the only swimmer in town. If there had been anyone else, he would have asked him to go to the studio in his stead, to make sure the paintings had not been swept away by the flood, since he was now feeling quite incapable of swimming so far. But to his renewed amazement he had no more company than Adam. So much so that he could have said, in retrospect, Darkness was on the face of the deep, and the spirit of Mark moved upon the face of the waters. . . . He made a last effort with all his muscles to push against the weight of the water, and at that very moment, he woke up.

What a dream! he thought, though he was greatly relieved all the same to be back in the real world. He went up to the window and drew back the curtain. It was still dark outside. The siren of the police car or the ambulance, which had apparently pierced his dream, could still be heard in the far distance.

When he went out, Mark was still burdened by the distress that his dream had left him with. At the door of the Town Café, where he made his regular call, a knot of men were talking about the sirens that he had just been hearing. "No, no," one of them was saying, "it can't be another holdup. In any case, there can't be much left to steal at that sorry branch! Ndrek must be right — they're testing the sirens on the cars that the Council of Europe sent us."

The barman, who seemed to assume that Mark was expecting his opinion, gave a twisted smile and said, "We'd like to be part of Europe, but up to now all we've got from Europe are those damned sirens! Aren't we lucky!"

Mark could feel someone come in the door behind him, breathing hard.

"Okay lads, you heard the news? Marian Shkreli . . ."

The man was panting for breath and could hardly speak.

"Well, what's happened to him, then?"

"He was shot as he came out of his front door. . . . That's what's happened to him!"

"Not possible!"

Mark was struck dumb for a moment. "Marian Shkreli has been shot. . . ." The sentence sounded blind and foreign, and he could not get it into his head. He wanted to yell, "But that's my boss!" as if this fact contradicted the news that had just been given out. For years, in fact, though he had no idea why, everyone had called him "boss" and had avoided using his surname. And now, on this fatal day, the boss's actual name had suddenly reemerged from oblivion to take its rightful place. Hardened and darkened by the blood that had been spilled, the name reattached itself to the body as it grew cold.

In no time at all the café filled with noise and bustle. Everyone was talking at the same time, without really bothering whether anyone else was listening.

"So that's what the wailing siren was about. I thought it might have been the fire engine. . . ."

Mark lit a cigarette and left without greeting anyone. He walked at a sharp pace and then broke into a run.

A small crowd had gathered in front of the block where the victim lived. The police car was parked at the curbside. The local magistrate and his team were also on-site, already busy taking photographs. Mark just stood there like the other onlookers, not daring to ask for details. He knew he would find it all out soon enough without having to ask. He would just have to keep his ear open to gossip.

Indeed, he caught up with the whole story very quickly. The director had been seriously wounded, and had been taken to the hospital. There was not much hope of saving him. A young man had fired a revolver at Marian as he came out of his front door. One single shot, to the forehead.

A single shot, Mark said over and again to himself, like a man in a daze.

Other people could now be seen converging on the spot from all directions. Asking the same questions, getting the same answers.

"The boss has been killed."

"You don't say! Who did it, and for what reason?"

"No idea. Maybe it was a crime of jealousy."

"But apparently it was more complicated than that, if you believe what people say."

"Oh, I see what you mean! A political murder! That's the fashion these days — people assume that some political score's being settled whenever someone has a stroke or gets buried in an avalanche."

"I don't think people will say that in this case. As far as I know, he wasn't involved in politics."

"By the way, which party did he support?"

"I have no idea. All I know is that the left thought he was right-wing, and the right thought he was left-wing."

"Poor man!"

Mark kept looking for the head of the music section in the ever-growing crowd. He didn't know what best to do — to follow his boss to the hospital or stay at the scene of the crime with the others. Then something made him shiver from head to toe. In the stream of ordinary conversations overheard, he thought he could make out a another language, a language of frozen expressions drifting like ice floes on the swell of the sea of chatter. Those old, cold ways of saying, quite distinct from the warm words of living speech, could now be heard ever more insistently. The victim's name — now preceded by the culprit's name — froze the blood in Mark's veins: *Angelin of the Ukaj hath slain Marian of the Shkreli.*

Mark felt his heart sink. The old formula left no room for doubt. This ancestral sentence had come out of the buried passages and clefts of the mountain and was now taking wing in the wide open. People in the crowd were still asking about the assassin in everyday language — So who is this Angelin Ukaj? What made him want to hit the boss? Why? . . . But the proud and unbending saying of old flew straight to the heart with its single, repeated message: *Angelin of the Ukaj hath slain Marian of the Shkreli.*

Mark thought he recognized the man in the felt hat whom he'd seen at that grim meeting in the warehouse. . . . He was observing the crowd with great attention, and it seemed to Mark that icy flames sprang forth now and again from the man's eyes. Mark's heart sank even further.

Someone took his elbow. It was his friend from the music section.

"Let's go to the hospital," he said. "The boss is supposed to be dying."

They set off at a brisk pace. Mark asked:

"So who is this Angelin Ukaj?"

He got no answer for a moment; then, in a burst, "I don't know. I heard a rumor that he was a fellow from the High Quarter. But what does it matter? He was only the *dorëras*, the hit man."

Mark shot a glance at his friend that seemed to say, So are you also part of the plot?

The head of the music section looked worried as he shook his head.

"It really is as if it was being reborn . . . the *Kanun*, I mean. Just what we needed!"

Mark would have liked to add, "And woe betide us!" but instead, his voice uttered words he had not even thought of: "You don't happen to know if this fellow has a sister?"

The other man shrugged his shoulders.

"No, I don't. I never even heard his name before."

There's a tough day ahead! thought Mark.

*   *   *

Shortly after noon the director of the Arts Center breathed his last in his hospital bed. Toward four, a small crowd gathered in the courtyard of the Arts Center, believing that the coffin would be brought there to lie in state. Inside the building, the telephone never stopped ringing, but that didn't mean people had any better idea of what had happened. In the end, someone from the town hall came to announce that the deceased, in accordance with his wishes, would be buried the next day in the village of his birth, Black Rock.

Nearly everyone who heard the announcement was dumbfounded. The boss wants to be buried in the mountains? For they had all forgotten that that was where he came from, and more precisely from the hamlet called Black Rock. Younger folk, who were not interested in general in where other people came from, would more likely have assumed that Marian had come to B—— from Tirana, not from the high plateau.

As they moved off, they talked about the way the boss had dressed, about his politeness and elegance, especially about those bunches of flowers he had delivered to his wife, just like a distinguished European. But some felt really disappointed as they made their way homeward. They would never have dreamed that a man so young, and so modern, could have come from such a desolate hole. Others just nodded their heads, gave a deep sigh, then, accustomed as they had been for so long to take nothing on trust, whispered in each other's ears, "Do you think the boss really wanted to be buried at Black Rock?" And then there were those who shook hands with acquaintances only to find out whether the bus really was going to leave from the town hall, and to check that it would not take more than an hour to get to Black Rock.

Mark had a cup of coffee at the bar of the Town Café and then went back up to his studio. He had a hunch that he would find a note from his girlfriend under the door. She hadn't shown her face since her uncle had turned up. "Don't fret, darling," she had told him. "As soon as he's gone, everything will return to normal. Just be patient."

With a flutter in his heart, he pushed open the heavy door. He forced himself not to look down to check if there was a piece of paper on the floor. But a strong intuition told him there wasn't.

He lit a cigarette and began to pace the room. He kept on walking up and down until his knees began to ache, and then he sat down.

The young woman arrived after night had fallen. He recognized her footfall on the stairs and stood at the door to greet her. Her face was white as a sheet. Without a word, she collapsed into his arms and burst into tears.

"My brother," she wailed between her sobs.

"It did occur to me," Mark replied. "I tried to banish the

thought of him from my mind, but I couldn't. Good God, the worst of our fears has come to pass!"

They both said the last sentence together. Unless, of course, they did not say it at all, but only thought it in unison.

He stroked her hair and tried to calm her down. But when she asked what would happen now, he had no answer to give her.

Right after the murder, the police had searched her family's home, but her brother had already gone into hiding. The whole business was full of contradictions: there was a highly public side to executions of this kind, yet the murderer was obliged to go under cover.

"It'll work out in the end," Mark said, looking as forlorn as ever. "There's got to be a solution. There always is."

They were sitting on the sofa. Mark kept turning his head toward the bay window. It was getting darker and darker.

The funeral procession drove very slowly along the mountain road. The hearse led the way, with a town-hall car following with the bereaved. Behind that was a jeep with NATO markings, a leftover from a recent mission to patrol the Kosovo border. There were two coaches, jam-packed with friends of the family, which could barely make the sharp curves. All of a sudden the tiny hamlet of Black Rock came into view, startlingly close up, as if seen through a zoom lens. Roofs, houses, windows, and the church with its recently repaired steeple stood out in the mist. It seemed so close you could touch it by stretching out your hand — but a moment later, after a hairpin turn in the mountain road, the village seemed to move off in a huff, into the far distance.

Farther on, the road dropped down before rising again. Black Rock, first seen up on high, almost in the clouds, now turned out to be deep down, lower than the rolling mist. A skittish place!

As he watched the landscape playing these games with the eye and the mind, Mark could not really concentrate on what the head of the music section was saying to him from the next seat in the coach. Black Rock now seemed to be dancing a crazy Irish reel.

The other passengers were talking at the tops of their voices, smoking like chimneys and coughing their hearts out.

"The killer made only the very slightest alteration to . . . how should I say . . . the outer dress of the execution ritual," Mark's friend and colleague explained to him. "Do you remember that grim meeting we went to? Where they were all adamant that the deed could only be done by a single shot? Well, the marksman kept to the rule: he fired only once. I've heard it said that he even called out to his victim before pulling the trigger. The question now is whether he's going to carry on with all the other rules from the *Kanun*, or stop short at this point. Did you see the two policemen who got into the other coach? I'm sure they're coming up to Black Rock to arrest the murderer if he turns up at the wake, as the old Code dictates."

"I doubt it."

"What do you doubt? That he'll come to the wake, or that he'll get arrested?"

"Both," Mark replied.

His friend pursed his lips. "You know, this business is getting more absurd every minute," he added after a pause. "None of it makes any sense."

"Of course. It was always that way."

Black Rock reappeared, and now it really was very close.

A passenger at the back was telling his neighbor that the poor man's wife hadn't wanted this highland burial at all, but in his very last moments, just before his dying breath, Marian had suddenly declared that such was his last wish.

"I think we're there, at last!" said the head of the music section.

The burial took place when the sun was at its zenith, as custom and ritual required. The two policemen looked dazed as they joined the procession. They had been given orders to arrest the murderer, even though, despite the rule of the *Kanun*, there was little chance that the latter would come to the funeral.

The men wailed the ancient lamentations, among which could be made out only the words "Woe betide us without thee, Marian Shkreli!" Following behind, the women sobbed, spoke of their memories, and sang the praises of the deceased.

A journalist, thin as a rake, whom Mark thought he had seen before, flitted to and fro among the mourners.

"As far as I know, the old custom only allowed men to shed tears. Isn't that so?" he mumbled.

Mark shrugged his shoulders.

"Are you working for the local paper?"

"Yes, I am. And to be honest I don't understand any of all this. The old customs they're supposed to be resurrecting are being trodden in the dust!"

Mark didn't respond, but the journalist kept on blathering just the same. He seemed to be talking to himself, or else dictating an article. His drone was constantly being interrupted by cries and wailing. The government of the left accused the right-wing opposition . . . of encouraging . . . a return to the *Kanun* . . . whereas the right . . . which pointedly called the victim a "beacon of democracy" . . . denounced the Communists . . . who, it contended, were trying to undermine national values . . . and the left responded to this accusation by saying that . . . whereas the right stressed the point that . . . Lord, what a shambles you have left us with, Marian Shkreli!

"And what does Spain have to do with all this?" The journalist stopped his droning, and addressed this question directly to Mark. "That's the second time the wailing women have mentioned Spain."

Mark too had picked up a phrase: "In that funereal land of Spain . . ."

"I don't know," he answered.

"Sounds like it has something to do with the death of the poor guy," the journalist said. "According to what I heard a few minutes ago, he really did make a trip to Spain. But whether that has any connection with his murder, I haven't the faintest idea."

"Same here," Mark admitted.

"It seems to me he went there to keep — or maybe to break — a promise. Do you think so too?"

"I really don't know," Mark replied. "As a matter of fact, he was a member of a delegation of the CNFR. . . ."

The journalist tried to make out the words that went with the lamentations of the bereaved, but the cool mountain breeze blew them away, and the effort made the young man's bony face look even more angular.

"In that funereal land of Spain? . . . Did you hear that? They said it again. It reminds me of that poem we had to learn at school, the 'Ballad of Ago Ymer.' Now, if I remember correctly, Ago was wilting away in a prison when he 're-ceived a piece of sad news' or 'had a funereal dream,' I can't quite recall. . . ."

Mark drifted off, as discreetly as he could, to get out of range of the unstoppable chatterer.

As a matter of fact, though, much the same thought had occurred to Mark. Marian's family must have heard of his trip to Spain, and they must have found it inexplicable, or at least puzzling. And since Spain played a role in the old "Ballad of Ago Ymer," they must have connected Marian's travel to the verses that had been handed on down the generations and had kept their truth for that very reason. In years to come, when they would tell the tale of Marian's death to their own grandchildren, they might well say, He went to a distant land called Spain, and there he had a dream foretelling his own death. . . .

The coffin was now being carried to the grave, and the crowd drew back all in one, like an ebbing wave.

Father Gjon gave a short oration, which he ended with the hope that the Albanians' troubled souls would at long last be visited by the peace of the Lord. Then the coffin was lowered into the grave. It was being covered with earth when Tom Kola, the longest-standing employee of the Arts Center, who sometimes stood in for the announcer or else acted the clown, shouted out, in a voice strangled by emotion, "Okay, Marian!"

Nobody understood the meaning of this interjection. It could have seemed a disrespectful joke at the expense of the deceased, except that Tom's eyes were red from weeping.

The funeral feast was laid out for the mourners when they came back from the cemetery to the house of Marian Shkreli's elder brother. The murderer did not turn up there either, and the two policemen, who now knew that they had come for nothing, sat at the end of the table, looking embarrassed. The murderer had clearly wanted to respect the ritual of execution to the letter, by firing a single shot, but he hadn't had the guts to take the old rules any further. That's what was said around the table.

"Just look over there," the head of music whispered in Mark's ear as they went into the guest room for coffee.

Mark looked where his friend was pointing, and what he saw astounded him. On the wall facing the door, over the fireplace, there hung the dead man's white shirt, with the "Boss" logo clearly visible. It was the old custom. It had two screamingly obvious bloodstains on it, one almost circular in shape, the other a meandering streak, like a mountain stream.

"I never imagined things could go that far," Mark's friend said softly. "The dead man's shirt hung out, just as it would have been four hundred years ago."

Mark opened his mouth to utter a response, but immediately shut it again, as if he was afraid that the sound it would make would come from another world.

Toward four in the afternoon, the friends of the slain man got back into the coaches to go home. Some were impressed by all the ritual; others, on the contrary, didn't try to hide their disappointment. There had been no request for a *bessa* for the murderer, and obviously no such offer had been made spontaneously. The murderer had undoubtedly observed some of the rules of the *Kanun*, but he'd turned a blind eye to many others. The dead man's family were tarred with the same brush. Someone declared, "Better to have no *Kanun* than to have the *Kanun* messed with!" Others took a different line and would have been content with an approximate application of the old rules, with a haphazard kind of tradition. Could you ask for more from something that had been dead and buried for fifty years?

That's how the conversation went in the coaches taking them all back down from Black Rock. People who thought these squabbles about ancient customs absurd kept their voices low as they chatted side by side. The fuss would drag on and on, they said, as it had with other Albanian lunacies of recent times. They reckoned that everyone involved was just play-acting, even without knowing it. Sure, they hung the dead man's shirt over the hearth, but it was a fair bet they had no idea of the real meaning of this old custom. And even if some of them had remembered, where could they still find people who knew how to read the messages from the dead that the bloodstains were supposed to contain?

Mark looked distractedly at the desolate wayside scenery. A sparse layer of fresh snow was making puny efforts to blanket the ground. On the way up to Black Rock he had scrutinized the landscape for a cave entrance or a cleft that might have been the way into the notorious deep storage depot. But now, because of the snow, he had no chance of making out anything of the sort.

He guessed that the head of the music section, who was sitting next to him, was thinking along exactly the same lines.

"I've often thought of what you told me," Mark said,

"about the head of state coming up here one night, to go through secret papers."

His friend nodded and then said, as if lost in thought, "All of them dive down deep to try to find something."

"All of them?" Mark repeated. Yes, that must be so. Some use a bloody shirt, others have recourse to ruses of various kinds, but they are all trying to get down to the bottom of it all, to the crime at the wellspring. Just like Oedipus.

The story of Oedipus, when it came to Mark's mind, always made him feel weary, for the poor king's tangle of troubles seemed as though it would never end. But no one had delved any deeper than he to discover the source and origin of his sinning. So deep, in fact, that he went right back to his mother's womb. Which is where he finally found his perdition. *Go fuck your mother!* That vulgar curse, uttered a thousand times, surely existed in every one of the Balkan tongues. Go back up your mother's cunt! . . .

Mark shook his head to dispel the drowsiness fogging his mind. Inside the coach, arguments had flared up anew. If the opposition wants to exploit this murder, my friend, then you can be sure the government will do likewise! The two sides have been copying each other like a pair of monkeys for a good long while. If one of them claims that the *Kanun* has just been used as a screen for the crime — then the other will, too. You can't rule that out, someone agreed. Woe betide the *Kanun*! . . . You should say, Woe betide Marian!

Well, yes, the real victim is certainly Marian, Mark thought. The poor man would have been utterly distraught to see the farce that was being made of his tragedy. But in circumstances like these, you can't be sure of anything. In his last extremity, he probably had renounced the trendsetter's mentality and manners that he'd adopted with his expensive shirts, loud ties, bouquets, and jolly "Okays." He probably had repented, and wanted to see his own blood debt taken back, tragically, the way it had been in ancient times.

Mark gave a deep sigh.

Black Rock had now dissolved in the far distance. But that did not prevent Mark imagining its reeling dance in the fog. And there was no one left who could say what it meant.

COUNTER-CHAPTER 5

MARK WAS AWAKENED all of a sudden by a disagreeable sensation. It resembled the kind of allergic itch that sleep does not soothe but only heightens. And that was how it turned out. After he had had his eyes open for a little while, the itching faded into a mere tickle.

It wasn't yet midnight, but Mark was not especially surprised by his sudden awakening after only an hour's sleep. It seemed quite natural, and it occurred to him that it was lucky he'd woken up, since he had so much to do. It would be great to use the quiet hours of the night to get things done, like slackers do, or people who like to make you think they're work zealots.

So he jumped out of bed, threw on some clothes, and went out. As he walked to the office, he felt icy cold. He knew there was a thick file of matters pending waiting for him, but he couldn't recall what they were. The walk to work seemed longer than usual, but that didn't surprise him either. Nor was he at all struck by the sign on the door. Instead of "Arts Center," it read "Police Station."

The night porter nodded a sleepy greeting. Mark bounded up the stairs, threw his office door open, and fell into the seat at his desk. The pending file was right there. A thick file. Dull gray. Whole pages of it came back to him all at once with a clarity of detail that left him astounded at his own power of recall. Of course, he had read the sheets over and over; he had thought about them so many times that he knew a fair number almost by heart.

Three men suspected of the holdup at the bank had been arrested two days earlier and were still maintaining their innocence. They freely admitted to being not entirely clean, but they insisted they had had nothing to do with this particular heist. They even took offense at being accused of such a vulgar crime. They could just about accept being suspected of an art theft, but as for robbing a bank . . .

Then they confessed to other misdemeanors. For instance, they said they had tried to rape an aunt of theirs, and also to make off with various works of art. . . .

"To hell with it, peccadilloes of that sort are chicken feed compared to the horrors that are going on in the country! You should put your time and energy into running down the big-time gangsters who run the government and parliament! They've got close ties with all sorts of mobsters, and with the Russian mafia too! Those are the people you should put in leg irons, not us! Anyway, there's no hurry, seeing as we're talking about old crimes."

"Time waits for no crime," Mark declared. He had questioned one of the guards of the former prime minister dozens of times, and he never could get anything at all out of a man who had been supposed to look after a leader who was killed, or else killed himself, twenty years earlier.

"I don't know what went on on the first floor of the residence," the man always replied. "My job was to look after the three doors on the ground floor, and I can swear to you that no one came in or went out."

"And who looked after the basement level?"

"The cellar? You mean the secret tunnel, the one that led to the house of the Comrade, the residence of the Great Guide? Are you really as ignorant as that, or are you just pretending? The tunnel had no guard because nobody would have dared spy on a passage leading to the house of the Guide. The reinforced door had a handle and bolt on one side only, on the Comrade's side, so that he alone could open it when he felt like it."

"Oh, I see. You mean that it was like the door that keeps Death from us, a one-way door you can only go through this way, and not that?"

"Yes, that's just how it was."

Mark felt weary in advance as he realized he wouldn't get anything more out of the man tonight, or any night. The case was as dead as the other one about the queen with rope marks around her neck. Between her two suicide attempts, she had made two confessions that contradicted each other entirely. In the first set of avowals, she had said unambiguously that her husband, Oedipus Rex, had never been her son. In the second confession, she admitted to having married her son, despite having known for many years that he had killed his own father. She had promised to explain everything at the next interrogation, but in the small hours of the appointed day, she managed at last to hang herself.

Files and yet more files, he thought. Instead of slowly getting clearer, the mysteries just thicken. The trial of Tantalus was now 102,000 years old, and the truth of it had been lost forever. Fortunately, investigations are done more quickly nowadays, but some of them could be awfully complicated: for instance, all the fuss the local Greens had been making over the killing of a house snake was far from calming down. The chief of police had poured oil on the fire when he had exclaimed without thinking, "We haven't got enough time to look after people, so why should we rack our brains over the death of a reptile?" The local press took it up with a few articles, and then investigators came down from Tirana, accompanied by a lawyer representing the Center for the Protection of Endangered Species, based in Munich. By all recognized definitions, the Balkan house snake belonged on the list of such species. Harsh punishment was demanded for such abuse. The defendants stood firm: they had neither killed nor abused the beast. It had died on its own, or, to be precise, it had frozen to death. Its carcass could be inspected at the morgue; they could do an autopsy if they wanted. It was in December, when snakes do freeze to death unless they are in the right conditions. Those said conditions had gone into decline — not just for snakes, but for the whole town. There were electricity cuts, and firewood was scarce. They weren't even able to heat the children's bedroom, so how could they manage to keep a snake warm?

You only had to dig a hole in the ground and put the snake in it, to hibernate. It would have slept through the winter, like all reptiles.

Well, you see, we didn't think of that. But anyway, the poor thing couldn't have known how to curl up underground, like his brothers. He was a house snake, a real rarity, as you yourselves said. . . .

And the rumors about . . . er, the stories about . . . your daughter, they're just vacuous gossip, I suppose? But even groundless chatter of that sort could have made somebody want to get rid of a snake, couldn't it?

Each time he got to this point in the investigation, Mark thought of the frozen snakes cut in two by the spades of the sappers clearing a way to the deep storage depot of the National Archives.

He was tempted to turn his mind to files dealing with less scandalous cases: a man wounded on the high plateau in a boundary dispute; a case of extortion and threats inside the town hall itself; the discovery of a prostitution ring strongly suspected of being based in Vlorë, the port nearest to Otranto. . . . But, for God knows what reason, he couldn't get the deep storage business out of his mind. Week after week he had kept on interrogating the only worker to have been arrested after the archive store had been closed. The others had slipped from his grasp. But the one they had shed hardly any light on the business. He just made it seem more mysterious.

"But you were actually present when the newly appointed head of state arrived late at night?"

"Sure, I was there."

"You must have been surprised to see him turn up like that, in the middle of the night, without any ceremony or fanfare, all alone with his two bodyguards?"

"Sure, it was unexpected, Your Worship."

"Especially as that particular April day had been very wearying for the head of state. The meeting of the Politburo that had given him supreme power had just finished. Urgent matters awaited his attention; the files were already on his desk. The whole country was still reeling from the late dictator's funeral. Europe had its eye on Albania, waiting to see what path it would follow. In the army, in the Sigurimi, among the malcontents, the mood was dark and deathly, and all sorts of rumors were spreading like wildfire. Most of them gave guesses about the composition of the next government. Other questions also required immediate answers. But in the midst of all this, the man took his two guards on a seven-hour drive, to trek up a mountain path all the way to your cavern. Bizarre, wasn't it?"

"It sure was, Your Honor."

"Presidents are not in the general habit of rushing through the night to consult the Secret Archives, are they? Especially not in the first hours of holding office, right?"

"No, they're not, Officer."

"So it must have made you curious. More than curious. What was this man looking for in such haste? Or should I say, in such a fluster? I suspect you wondered, didn't you?"

"I don't know how to explain. Of course, I admit that it puzzled me, but, to be honest, it didn't plunge me into the kind of anxiety you seem to imagine. I thought it must be one of the things that are ordinary for people belonging to higher circles. And that's all."

"All the same, once you became aware of the puzzling nature of the event, you must have paid attention, and you did, didn't you? So whether you like it or not, you tracked the comings and goings of your august visitor."

"Of course."

"So can you tell us what they were, precisely?"

"The ones where I was actually present, you mean?"

"Of course, the ones you observed . . . Do you mean there were other things happening that you didn't actually see?"

"Of course there were. . . . Neither I nor anyone else could have observed what he did in the Bat Room."

"The Bat Room, I understand, has the highest security rating in the entire deep storage depot?"

"That's right. We call it the Bat Room because a bat once got into it. Up to that time, in fact, the room had no name."

"Please go on. . . . If I understand you correctly, the head of state, once he got into the deep storage facility, asked to be taken to that room?"

"Quite so."

"Without even stopping at the office of the director of the archives? Without even saying 'Good evening, Comrade' to you?"

"That's how it was, sir."

"Then do go on. Try to remember exactly each of the president's acts and movements."

"Well, I'll try. He took a piece of paper out of his pocket, looked at it, and it was then that he asked to be taken to the notorious Bat Room. All the while I kept my eye on the small crowd that had gathered at the metal barrier door. Then the director took two keys from his pocket, and turned one after the other in the two keyholes in the door. There was a third key — but that was one the president himself brought with him. That key was always kept in Tirana, at the Center. So the president took it out and opened the door."

"And then?"

"He pushed the door open, went into the Bat Room, and closed the door behind him. And after that, nobody can say what went on. Everyone else, including the bodyguards, stayed outside. After a while, the head of state opened the door an inch or two and asked for the director. So the director went in, but came out again after only a couple of minutes. We all just stood there, in silence, at the door."

"And then?"

"And then, nothing. Our visitor spent nearly three hours in the secret room. He was white as a sheet when he came out. He left with his bodyguards without saying a word. It must have been around 3:00 A.M."

"So he was white as a sheet when he came out. He came out looking white after spending three hours searching for something. And he left for Tirana immediately. Didn't that puzzle you? Give you insomnia? Make you want to scream inwardly, 'This is an enigma! A dark and mysterious enigma!'?"

"Well, sure it did. We're human beings too, you know. The whole thing struck us all, but maybe not as hard as you say, when you call it a dark and mysterious enigma or whatever."

"Really? I see! You don't like things to be 'mysterious,' then?"

"I didn't say that."

"What was in the secret file? Answer me!"

"But I have no idea! I've never even seen it."

"Has anybody seen it? Answer!"

"No, nobody has seen it."

"What do you mean, nobody? Someone must have worked on it. Someone must have brought it to the archive, someone must have filed it, someone must have put in the page numbers. Answer!"

"Well, yes, someone did work on it."

"But you just said nobody had seen it!"

"All right, all right, there was someone, and his name was Shpend Simahori, but he is no longer of this world. He

drowned last year in the Strait of Otranto, when he was trying to get to Italy."

"Aha, the Strait of Otranto! You can lose a lot of things in
the big wide sea! When you're looking for someone you
really have to find, you never have to wait very long for that
familiar tune to come on again: He's down with Davy Jones,
at the bottom of the Adriatic Sea! Now listen to me! This is
my last question. Look me straight in the eye and answer!"

"Yes, sir."

"Did you ever hear of some strange, not to say horrible,
photographs in the files stored down in the Bat Room?"

"No, sir."

"Keep your eyes on mine! . . . Did you ever hear tell of a
snapshot of the Politburo, standing over the corpse of one
of their present or former colleagues, with guns in their
hands, delivering the coup de grâce? Answer!"

"No, sir."

"Did you ever see a photograph of the new head of state
firing a gun at the lifeless body of a former member of the
Politburo?"

"Oh, no, sir!"

"And you did not see the selfsame president looking for
that photograph in particular, on that night in April, down
in the Secret Archives? This is your last chance. Answer!"

"Oh, God, I would have done far better to drown in the
Adriatic!"

. . . Mark held his forehead in the palms of his hands.
This inquiry was wearing him out like no other inquiry ever

had. He looked at the clock. It was 3:00 A.M. There was still some time to go.

The whole business was like an infinite set of cogs: files within files within files, with no end to it. He stayed for a long while with his head in his hands, without moving. Then, like a diver who fills his lungs before jumping in, he took a deep breath and plunged back into the paperwork on his desk.

The forgers of the *Book of the Blood* . . . The only real exhibit that had been found so far was a copy of a memorandum of agreement with a group of Germans (the very same people were suspected of having manufactured Hitler's diaries). The Germans, for their part, clung unwaveringly to the explicit content of the memorandum, which was, they said, an understanding about a pipeline project. An inexperienced eye could indeed believe such a story, since the memorandum did seem to refer to the construction of an aqueduct.

But what was the real meaning of Clause 7, which stipulated that "the Albanian side is responsible for drawing up the text, while the German side takes responsibility for technical aspects"? What text?

"The text" was the wording that was supposed to be put on the commemorative plaques that they planned to erect in places where murders had been committed in disputes over water rights. "You are not unaware, we assume, that water has often given rise to violent conflicts."

"Are you a pipeline construction enterprise, or historians of rural life?"

"Assistant Commissar, sir, aqueducts are often the focus of painful memories."

"And Appendix Two? 'Draft Text, p. 714. The Ballideme family has a blood to claim from the Kryezeze. The Frangaj family has a blood debt to the Hoti. The Prejlocaj family owe an injury to the Shkreli. Gjon Pal Marku has a blood debt. The Berisha and the Nano families have no claim on each other. The Krasniqi clan has blood to claim from the Gurazi . . . ,' and so on and so forth! How do you account for all that? Do you have the gall to claim that all this is just wording for commemorative plaques?"

"That is exactly what it is, Deputy Commissioner, sir."

"Stop all this rubbish! And tell me honestly what the purpose of this so-called *Book of the Blood* really is. Who commissioned it from you? To what end? To have the whole of Albania descend into chaos and mayhem? Tell me!"

. . . but nobody's going to speak out, Mark thought. The twenty-six painters who'd helped put Gentian in jail refused to talk, and so had the politicians who were linked to the outlawed gangs, and so had the travelers who'd talked to the Sphinx at the gates of Thebes. Did you see it all with your own eyes, or did fear and terror cause you to see nothing at all? What went on in your mind to turn the political tension that was perceptible all around — that well-known foreboding that is always the prelude to a dictatorship — to turn that tension, in your mind, into a Sphinx? Or perhaps you belonged to a faction eager to put Thebes under a rule of iron? And to favor this plan, were you not yourself involved in provoking the fear and anxiety that in the end created the Sphinx?

Those are supertough cases to solve, thought Mark. They'll never be cracked. It would be easier to get to the bottom of the iceberg that sank the *Titanic,* or of NATO's C-in-C, or of an avalanche that feels bruised by the cadaver it carries down the mountainside within it.

"But you at least don't need to wear me out!" he said in his own mind to his girlfriend, even while asking her for a confession.

"I don't understand why you suddenly want to question me on a subject that never seemed to interest you very much — how I lost my virginity, and to whom. Was it our gym teacher, the first man to see us in underwear, when we were twelve or thirteen? Or was it one of my cousins, on some long hot summer afternoon, when we were all lying on the grass, pretending to sleep, but with all our senses on fire? Why are you so anxious to know the answer, Mark? It was one or the other, or maybe both. . . ."

"What sort of an answer is that? Why so vague? Why?"

"Because it's better that way, Mark. Believe me, my darling, it's better that way."

The gym teacher, or a cousin during a heat wave . . . Incest seemed to be the latest thing!

A shudder like the one that had awakened him made him look toward the window. His nostrils flared, as if he had smelled something intoxicating. No more time! he could hear himself screaming, silently.

He slammed shut the file in front of him, threw on his overcoat, and ran down the stairs just as fast as he had come up.

In the pale light of dawn, the city seemed quite foreign. He was only walking, but he panted as if he had been racing along. Suddenly his house rose before him, as quickly as if he had run there. He glided up the stairs, opened the door, and fell onto his bed fully dressed, as if he had been felled by lightning. He had just enough lucidity to think that epileptics must crumple like that after they've had an attack, and then he fell into a deep, deep sleep.

CHAPTER 6

MARK SPENT ALL OF SUNDAY MORNING at his easel. He couldn't recall another occasion when he had taken such pains to mix a color. He paused to look at the stains his oils had made on his hands and sleeves, and all over his smock as well. What he was trying to get was a particular shade of white, as cold and transparent as possible. Without that white he would never be able to represent the sunken part of the iceberg on a canvas. In one corner he had inscribed, "A History of the Void," and beneath it, "Eight Views of the Iceberg that Sank the *Titanic.*"

He looked once more at the paint stains on his smock. They seemed so cold that he imagined he was covered in sleet, and shivered at the thought of it. That was a good sign. But even so, he wasn't really satisfied.

To figure the submerged part, the part of the iceberg that

had to look blurred and immaterial, like a waking dream, but which was also the most tragic and sinister part: that was what he found desperately difficult to do.

He couldn't say on what day or at what time he'd had the idea of painting the curriculum vitae, so to speak, of the nameless iceberg that had caused so much sorrow, through eight different views of it. What had intrigued him about the tragedy of Marian Shkreli, or so it seemed, had been its well-spring, its root cause. In his mind, as if in a hall of mirrors, it had appeared first as a shroud of fog; then as black propaganda; then as a cause that was not what it seemed; then as age-old nonsense and stupidity; then, finally, as pure contingency, which, like a tiny snowball, had been quite enough to set off an avalanche. His mind easily made the jump from avalanche to iceberg: both came from far away — from the high peaks or from the Arctic wilderness; both required sub-zero temperatures; both were never named; both brought random death (an avalanche can bury a village, an iceberg can sink a liner); and, to clinch the equivalence, both disappeared without leaving a trace, save for human pain and fear.

Mark's first sketches showed the uncle's lonely walk down the mountain, the naked body of the girl at the heart of the tragedy, the distraught features of the brother chosen to carry out the execution. But he put these aside and transferred all the human features of the story to the iceberg. He saw it as a bull, the leader of a herd, with ice-calves in its train alongside the female floes of the clan. The long trek to the North Atlantic, a fruitless drifting that would bring it face-to-face with an immense floating palace of light and music. Blindly, it locked its horns on the ship. When the deed was done, nobody gave a further thought to the old bull. It was still there, standing erect in the water whence the frozen corpses were fished up, but it occurred to nobody to mark it in any way — with a branding iron, for example, as criminals were marked in the Middle Ages, or if not by such a weal, then at least with some other sign, like a half-raised flag, a black sheet, or just a cross.

The iceberg went the way it had come: namelessly, just a bull in a herd of cattle, with nothing more to say about it. Perhaps it drifted northward again with a great gash in its side, like a war wound from its one single adventure in the world of human beings. The rest of its life among fellow bergs must have been as dull and colorless as it had been before the southern excursion, just like everything else that you could say about it. In old age it would have begun to shrink, and in the end it would have merged with the ice cap, to universal indifference, while some of its younger clansmen would be setting off for far horizons, toward the very place where it had once brought death and destruction.

Mark thought someone had knocked at his door. It was his girlfriend, but he had been so buried in his painting that, for the first time in his life, he hadn't heard her footsteps coming up the stairs.

He kissed her ebulliently; she responded in kind. They had not seen each other for three weeks. He whispered sweet nothings in her ear, but couldn't stop himself from confessing what he had resolved not to say to her at all: that after all that had happened, he had been afraid that she would never come back to him. Then, since she asked him what he had been doing, he tried to explain it all as best he could. So, my brother looks like an iceberg? she said, trying to make it sound like a joke. No, not your brother, but your uncle, and actually, less your real uncle than the *Kanun* itself, or to be more precise, the essence of the *Kanun*, which is really ineffable . . . He realized that the more he tried to explain what he was doing, the less sense it made.

"I just can't explain it!" he burst out in the end, with a laugh. "To do that, I would have to be as logical as ice. . . . But hang on, it's getting rather chilly in here. I'll just light the stove."

When the stove was roaring nicely, Mark opened the lid and moved the bed over toward it.

He had imagined that the whole highland folk story would have bored her, but in fact it produced the opposite effect. Color came to her cheeks, she couldn't hide her desire to hear more about it. He stroked her breasts, then, burning with desire, he looked at her hairless underarm. As he got a condom out of the drawer in the bedside cabinet, she held his hand and whispered in his ear, as if it was a great secret:

"There's no need. I'm on the pill."

*   *   *

As usual, after lovemaking they began to talk about what they should properly have discussed beforehand, but which desire had set aside or made seem unimportant. Her brother had been in hiding since the day of the shooting. A kind of muffled calm had descended on her family. The contraceptive pills, well, they'd come from a cousin of hers, who'd got them from Tirana. . . . Strange to say, the unprecedented circumstances at home had not dulled her sexual desire but had sharpened it. I guess you noticed that, she said, kissing him on the nape of his neck. He let her know he agreed and was ready to have another go. . . . This time was really sublime, she said. She took the cigarette from Mark's fingers, drew deeply on it twice, and then realized she needed to wash up.

She went home before dusk. From the bay window, Mark watched her walking away. He wondered whether a woman's bearing was different after she'd made love, but found no answer to the question. Without you, he thought a moment later, I have no answer to anything. He tried to imagine her sexual parts changing shape in time with her step. How many times — especially when he was suffering the pangs of desire — had he attempted to draw those private parts, without ever quite being satisfied with his drawings? There was always something missing. And as soon as he tried to get it down on paper, he invariably left out some other trait. He knew it wasn't a great discovery of his own, but he was convinced that the reason for this was that the invisible part of a woman's sex — like the unseen part of an iceberg — was the most important. Obviously it was the hidden part that gave it all its value. A street poet whose couplets were circulated by word of mouth had called a woman's genitalia "a wolf howling in winter under thickly falling snow."

Mark shivered with cold as he strode toward the Town Café. He'd noticed there was a special atmosphere in it whenever the chief of police came to have a drink there. On this occasion, he was with the recently appointed prosecutor, and as a result, gossip about the imminent arrest of the bank robbers, as well as more intense recent hopes of capturing Marian Shkreli's assassin, flew around the barroom from table to table. But though they had these two things very much in their minds, the customers were laughing about something else.

Mark ordered his coffee and tried to stop himself from smiling. That was something he often had to do in this café, when, upon entering, he became aware of inspiring a kind of awe that he thought inappropriate. Sometimes he even felt guilty about coming in and freezing what had been a jolly and relaxed atmosphere in the café. The faces of all these good folk, who till then had been speaking quite freely — telling each other scabrous jokes about parliamentary debates or female buttocks — suddenly stiffened, as if they had been caught in the act. Good God, they imagine I've got huge ideas going round in my head, Mark said to himself. Whereas in fact there are only puny little thoughts between my ears, and not even very logical ones. . . . If his mind ever pulled itself together, it was only thanks to these people.

As he took small, slow sips of his coffee, he tried but in the end failed to stop his mind from wandering back to his young girlfriend's body. The outer appearance of the slit between her legs gave no hint of the wild beast screaming in its hidden folds — like a plain-faced and simpleminded guard stationed at the entrance of the treasury. It was even reminiscent of the approach to the deep storage depot (if that was what Mark had seen), with thick bushes hiding the entrance. In any case, what happens inside is inexplicable, Mark thought, and it's not by chance that Oedipus got lost in that inner darkness.

"What's really a priority," someone at the next table said, "is for people to get their teeth seen to! You may smile, but I've been thinking about this for a long time!"

Mark smiled too, but the speaker continued with his thoughts. "If you want to give a short but serious snapshot of the Communist world as a whole, you couldn't do better than likening it to a gathering of thousands and thousands of people with bad teeth."

"Ah, so you think I should know how to put it all right? Some say start by reestablishing public order, others say stick to the rules laid down by the World Bank, or else start by repairing the roads — but you, you say that the real priority is people's teeth! Boy, you've got some great ideas!"

"So you, sir, do you really believe all the things you just listed are actually more important than teeth? Don't make me laugh! Benighted as you are, you can't possibly realize that the two Germanys, East and West, which were apparently swooning with the desire to unite, are about to split up again, over the question of teeth! So you didn't know, did you? You've got rotten teeth, we can't live in the same state as people like you! That's what the Wessies have started to grunt and mumble. . . ."

"Now tell me just where you picked up that piece of nonsense!"

"None of your business. But the story was on the radio and in the papers, too."

Within a minute the conversation had drifted on to something else and Mark lost the thread of it. His eyes wandered automatically toward the alcove, where the chief of police and the public prosecutor were sitting. When his glance crossed theirs, he imagined — for the briefest instant — that light flashed between them. His foreboding that they would one day put him through interrogation — or that he would interrogate them — was so powerful that it would have seemed quite natural to him if he had stood up, gone straight over to their table, and said, Look, if that's what you plan to do, why not get on with it right now? We can pull straws to see who goes first. . . . Mark sincerely felt no apprehension about such a turn of events. It would not have occurred to him to complain to the Human Rights Watch, in Helsinki or in Tirana. He was anxious to find out what the style of the interrogation would be. He didn't think much had changed in this kind of exercise since Zeus had begun to put Tantalus through questioning. So the police chief could get on with it. But he shouldn't expect any quarter from Mark, when it would be his turn to do the questioning. An artist can be as cruel as anybody else. If not more so . . .

At the next table, a new set of customers had taken the places of the previous drinkers. A well-established conversation on the prospects of a war in Kosovo was in train. Hostilities would break out next winter, no doubt about it. This assertion was hammered out with such force that two of the drinkers seemed to shrink under the blow, bearing the signs of a battle that had not yet hit them.

Mark felt he had to get up and leave this evil café. No, no, he thought, I haven't done anything to deserve that! And it was true that he didn't deserve to have liberty, for which he had waited with such fervor for so many years, come to him in the form of lunacy.

The cold outside did him good. As he walked toward home, he passed the town hall, past the corner of the building where official death notices were posted. He stopped for a while to read them, one by one, but in an odd way doubting the truth of each. He was convinced that the number of people who for one reason or another have themselves declared dead though they are still alive was on the increase. It was already four years since a friend of his from Tirana, passing through this small town, had told him that he intended to disappear for a while, if he could earn enough money for it. "It's safer that way. I plan to settle in Canada, or else have myself declared dead."

Before taking the turn into his own street, he strolled around the empty square that looks onto the park. Zef's windows seemed lit, though very faintly. Mark took cautious steps, as if he feared that a clumsy footfall might extinguish the light in the window. But that's what happened a few minutes later — Zef's light went out. He thought for a moment that it might be coming back on, but it wasn't a light, properly speaking. It was more like a pale reflection of the lantern of a cart coming down from the highlands. But that glimmer also quickly disappeared.

It was then that he became sure that a new species of human being — able to move from the light to the underworld and back again — was already among us, in large numbers. They had no name for the time being, but they probably soon would. For instance, they could be called the unliving, or else the undead.

Two or three times he recalled the icy gleam in the eyes of the chief of police. You could not dismiss the possibility that the policeman had thought Mark was a member of the new race.

Mark tried to remember with whom he might have discussed the theft of immortality by Tantalus, but it made him laugh at himself. A conversation of that kind would indeed have made the secret policemen of old prick up their ears, because the words *immortal* and *immortality* were not often used outside the context of the Supreme Leader. But all that had ceased to be imaginable. Nowadays, the most that Mark could be suspected of was involvement in the holdup of the bank at B———.

Counter-Chapter 6

THE STRAIT OF OTRANTO . . . Where all lie in peace . . .

There are hundreds of us down here. Some called out to the Virgin Mary as we sank; others invoked Allah, Jehovah, or even Buddha. We are Ukrainian, or Chinese, or Moldovan, or Kurdish, or Italian; and some of course are Albanian.

In our unlife, you might think everything was over, that nothing happens anymore. But you would be wrong. There is never an end, just like there never really was a beginning.

Even down here in the murky depths, something is always going on. Children float down and drown; their transparent hair refracts a mysterious light, like the glow of jellyfish. Other bodies inexplicably rise to the surface — maybe because they have lost weight to carnivorous fish — and their mutilated forms bob around on the waves as if beset by doubt.

All about, innumerable inanimate objects and the out-
lines of animate beings jostle for space: tin crutches, silver
neck chains that have slipped off emaciated necks, homo-
sexuals in stunned embrace, glass eyes, candles, dolls, dock-
side cats pursued down to the lower depths by ghosts of
tigers, crash helmets, a stone from the Berlin Wall inscribed
with "A Souvenir of Andy, a refugee," slimy condoms looking like ordinary mollusks, low-denomination dollar bills,
hymn books, taillights from a police car, old boots, deter-
gents, alphabet books, and finally, an unexploded NATO
bomb, which will surely spread panic. . . .

So that after you too have passed through the clutter, the
whole mess — transparent children, crutches, gays, the stop
sign, the tiger ghost, coffins, hymnaries, eels, champagne
bottles — reappears in a different order.

A polished silver mirror thrown in from who knows
where — maybe by Death herself, whom in our blindness
we think invisible, but who walks in our midst.

And so our wailing — simultaneously a plea, a lament,
and a curse — fills every part of this watery grave. O Strait
of Otranto, may you be dammed and dry up to nothing! Let
the sun consume you! And may cartloads of salt and mortal
poison be heaped upon you until the end of time!

CHAPTER 7

JUDAS HAD REAPPEARED IN B——. This time, he was alone. He spent Friday night at the hotel, then, after breakfast, went back up to his ice-cold room. It was rumored that the names of the writers he had denounced, along with those of the refugees who had recently escaped to Germany, would soon be published.

He had been seen the previous Saturday, rucksack on his back, making his way along the road leading out of town. Apparently it was the rucksack that made everyone assume that, like most Germans, whose manners he had adopted, Judas had taken up country rambling at the weekend. It had become a fixture in the town of B——, and Cuf Kertolla had even declared portentously that it was easier to strike a German dead with a single blow than to keep him shut up in town at the weekend.

ISMAIL KADARE

Others, who had become universally skeptical in recent years, to the point where no proverb or poem could dispel the dark clouds that constantly gathered in their minds, thought it more prudent to drink up their coffee and go see with their own eyes whether this *Wanderung* was simply an exercise in the German manner or a walk of a different kind.

They came back not long after with a look of triumph on their faces, saying that they had been right: just as they suspected, Judas had made his way to the higher ground, to the place where people believed the deep storage depot of the National Archives was still to be found.

So that's what was up!

This discovery, which would have sounded quite dramatic only a little while before, was repeated around town, only in a tone of mild disappointment. In recent months, so many people had poked around the area where the Secret Archives were supposed to be stashed that the fact that Judas had been up there as well seemed unsurprising, even banal.

Once the first wave of archive hunting subsided, the fever resumed that spring, together with the seasonal improvement in the weather. The movement was set off by a pair of rascals from the nearby village, who had been stalking a couple of tourists, hoping to see them indulging in open-air frolics. They were disappointed: the tourists took some maps out of their backpacks and started walking around in circles like a pair of simpletons. That was all it took to reignite the old obsession and to revive the memory of its now-distant origin — the visit, many years before, of the newly appointed head of state.

Around the place where the archives were supposed to be hidden, all sorts of people could be seen every day, or almost every day, especially on weekends. There were day trippers pretending to be on a picnic; people from Tirana who claimed to want to admire the view of the early autumn snow on the peaks; others claiming to be there for a rendezvous, or members of religious sects, or even geologists. Some of them seemed agitated and jumpy; others looked desperate, as if suffering some inner torment; and yet others wept in silence. There was no way of distinguishing between those who had come to hide something and those there to find something hidden. Smooth-faced, bespectacled tourists would suddenly drop their amiable smiles and reach into their packs for digging tools they had camouflaged in a variety of unsuspected ways — inside boxes of spaghetti, mountain boots, even a violin!

It was said that the ground around the site was a honeycomb of pits and tunnels, but that was perhaps only the fruit of journalists' unbridled imaginations. In any case, no one could recall such an invasion of visitors since the time when new chrome ore deposits had been discovered in the area, a moment when, to its great surprise, Albania found itself the world's third-largest producer. The national daily reported on the excitement gripping the little northern town of B—— by recalling the old diggers' rush with a pun on the word *chrome*. Under the headline "Chrome Diggers Become Crime Diggers," the paper pointed out that the exploration fever that had now seized the little town for the second time was spreading to other parts of Albania, more specifically to those other areas where there were reasons for supposing that the Secret Archives might be tucked away. The article ended with a question: Had there really been a deep storage depot at B——? Was it located somewhere else? Did it really exist at all?

Mark was highlighting the last sentence in the paper when he heard a child's stifled scream coming from behind his chair:

"Sir! Sir!"

He turned around and saw a Gypsy boy, of the kind who regularly came to beg in the café. The lad asked for some small change, which Mark gave him. But the beggar boy didn't go away. He kept trying to say something with his hands.

"Get lost!" Mark ordered. "Enough's enough!"

The ragamuffin put his mouth to Mark's ear and whispered a few words. Mark could make out only a few, and those with some difficulty: a girl . . . on the corner . . . looking at the poster . . .

Mark raised his open hand.

"Are you going to get lost, or do you want this across your face?"

Mark was astounded that the Romany didn't give the slightest sign of being scared.

"Don't be angry, sir, I'm not a pimp. It's your girlfriend who's sent me. She's waiting for you on the corner."

Mark jumped up, paid for his coffee, strode across the room, and as soon as he was outside, began to run.

He could see the girl from a long way off. She was indeed waiting at the corner, pretending to look at the film posters.

"I'm sorry to disturb you," she said before he could get a word in. "I've been looking for you all over."

"What's happening? Tell me quickly!"

"Nothing of what you might think. Only I really need you now. It's urgent; I just had to see you right away."

"So tell me!"

"I can't speak here. I'll come to your studio this evening."

"This evening? In other words, tonight?" Mark said, not without surprise.

They had never spent a night together, even though Mark had often dreamed of it.

She nodded.

"Yes, this evening, and until late, as late as possible."

Mark couldn't believe his ears.

"So you'll spend the night with me?"

She sighed deeply.

"I beg you, please, don't ask for details!"

She seemed to be finding it hard to express herself. Mark said:

"Okay, okay, I won't ask any more."

"Good. Wait for me in the studio until late, maybe even after midnight."

He could barely stop himself from asking her what this was all about, but he had never seen her looking so forlorn.

They started walking side by side without a word. The street was littered with autumn leaves; oddly enough, the leaves seemed to assuage their fears.

"Now I have to go," she said. She took two steps, and then turned around. "My darling, believe me, I can't tell you anything else. . . . When we meet again, you'll see I'm right."

He forced a smile, then watched her as she walked away with a gait that, it seemed to Mark, disguised some guilty secret.

"When we meet again, you'll see I was right," he muttered to himself, repeating her words over and over.

He expected to be lost in speculation about the nature of the mystery, but to his great surprise his mind — which usually raced off in excitement at the slightest provocation — found itself utterly calm. For the time being, he was even surprised that the scene that had just taken place had not happened much earlier. There had been so many circumstances that could have led her to say, I am in terrible trouble, wait for me on the stroke of midnight!

In his mind, several different scenarios jostled each other clumsily: she was running away from home; her brother had threatened suicide; she was pregnant; her fearsome uncle had returned; she wanted him involved in negotiations to patch up the quarrel; she was trying to get hold of a visa (rather than just making an application) so that her brother could seek refuge in Switzerland. . . . Mark proceeded slowly along the icy street. The sight of the bare poplars was as restful to his eyes as the dead leaves on the ground, if not even more relaxing.

How ghastly! Mark sighed as he stood in front of the bay window of his studio. He'd never before seen time slowing down in the shape of a fat and dawdling mammoth. He'd used all the regular tricks to make time flee faster — walking around town, puttering about with odd jobs he'd been putting off for ages, painting, rolling his own cigarettes, dropping off for a snooze. . . . Not only did they have no effect on the mammoth, they appeared, for the most part, to produce the opposite result.

When evening came, he made a kind of discovery: daytime waiting was different from waiting at dusk, which in turn was distinct from a nighttime vigil. He still had to experience the most acute form of the latter state, when all his waiting would condense as at the leading edge of a comet: waiting after midnight.

Since he had prepared himself for it, the last stage of waiting turned out to be less dreary than he had imagined. Sheer fatigue numbed his senses somewhat, so that the first minutes after midnight seem to pass quite quickly.

When he heard her coming up the stairs, the first thing that occurred to him was that his girlfriend was not alone.

But his brain was in no state to process it, and only when he opened the door and saw the figure standing behind the girl did he almost exclaim, I thought as much!

"My brother Angelin," she said.

Now he was sure he had guessed correctly. The boy's thin, badly shaven face matched in every particular the visage he had often imagined. Yes, of course, he had guessed! Just as he had intuited that his girlfriend, like most Albanian women, more than a wife or a mistress, was first and foremost a *sister*.

His first thought after closing the door was to go and take down the nude for which she had sat. Though the face was still only sketched in, he felt that the other man would also be able to identify her by her sexual organs. He must be familiar with them. He must have seen his sister. Maybe he had even touched her, some summer afternoon. . . . That pill she had taken at an unexpected time, when she was in distress about her brother . . . My God, maybe it wasn't so much the fear of getting pregnant as the unconscious terror of consanguinity that had pushed her toward the pill?

"Sit down, please," Mark said to the two of them, thinking inwardly, What a mess we're in! Then: "You must excuse me, if I seem distracted, but you can understand that . . ."

"Of course," the young woman said. "We are too. Angelin and I wanted first of all to ask you to forgive us for disturbing you at such a late —"

"No matter," said Mark.

He would have liked to add that he thought it quite natural that they should turn to him, but he immediately saw that if the young man was unaware of their relationship, then there was no reason for Angelin to find it natural.

He remembered the bottle of schnapps. It was like a life buoy, and he busied himself for a moment with getting it and some glasses out of the cupboard.

"Mark," she said, with her eyes steady on him. "We have come about something very important."

"I was sure you had," he replied.

She took a deep breath. He quickly realized that only she would speak. The brother and the sister must have gone over the issue many times together, he thought, for hours on end, side by side. . . .

What she said turned out to be a bit of a muddle. Conventional ways of saying things seemed not much use in the context. Rather the opposite: instead of opening up new lines of thought, they seemed to block things off. Her brother had killed, in circumstances that were obscure. Contrary to what many people thought, he had not been pressured into committing the act by some devotee of the ancient *Kanun* — such as their uncle. It was sheer chance that made their uncle's four-day stay coincide with the period of deep distress that Angelin had gone through. If they had had a different visitor at that time — say, the leader of a Japanese or Tibetan sect, a collector of weapons for Kosovo, an Irish Republican, or a member of a secret society recruiting suicide bombers to rid the world of dictators — then Angelin's fate might also have been quite different. But what came up was the *Kanun*, and he had been entranced by it. It really was bad luck that news of the Kosovo uprising had been so long in coming, just like the reply from the Association of Young Idealists in Tirana.

During his stay in Tirana the previous spring, he had suffered his first great shock. He'd been out every evening with his cousins and their friends, crawling from bar to dive and from bingo hall to gambling den. His rejection had come in stages. At first, he thought that the money talk would eventually run out and give way to other subjects of discussion. But night after night the talk of money resumed, ever more anxious, more desperate, smothering everything else and becoming, in the end, suffocating. After so many years of tightened belts, his sister said, to justify this state of affairs, it was perfectly normal that people should be greedy for material satisfactions. But Angelin could not get used to it. Such greed seemed to him an ill omen. On his fourth evening in the capital, he invented an excuse for not going to bingo. The next day he did not even want to go outside. I know what you're feeling, his sister told him then. And she'd told him about the Association of Young Idealists, as she'd come across two of its members quite by chance. The same afternoon, the four of them got together at the Piazza Café. He listened patiently to the Idealists as they laid out their program, and then opined that a more radical plan of action was needed. He admitted he had always been slow in reacting to events. His favorite hero was Jan Palac, the Czech who had set fire to himself to protest the Russian occupation, but he had never had the opportunity to do anything similar: he was only fourteen when the Communist regime had fallen. After that, things had changed in such a confusing way that he had found it difficult to know how to orient himself. He was ready to join their organization and to carry out any of its orders. If they decided to issue warnings to corrupt ministers of state, and then to members of parliament, for instance, and if these high and mighty folk did not give up their ignoble ways, then he was prepared to put the threats into effect, with his own hand . . . that is to say, to carry out the first murder!

The two Idealists were dumbfounded. They declared they had never gone so far as to envisage action of that kind. In any event, they would give him an answer on that point later.

Angelin returned to the North and waited in vain for the Idealists' answer. His eyes became ever hollower. He spoke less and less. And that was when the uncle from the country came on his visit. He too was full of rancor and deeply disappointed. In his view, the country was going to the dogs. Decline and decay were everywhere to be seen. Courage and honor, which he had expected to be reinvigorated by the fall of Communism, were losing ever more ground. The only hope lay in the resurrection of the old customary law. The *dorëras*, the executioners, had been the flower of the country's youth. Unlike their counterparts today, who played bingo until dawn, the *dorëras* had gone bravely toward their own death. . . . Angelin listened to this talk with utter disdain.

He had never had any particular respect for the *Kanun*, and he would no doubt have continued listening to his uncle in the same way, that is to say, with indifference, if in the flood of the old man's words there hadn't been three or four that struck him and entered his head like well-aimed nails. Those young executioners, the country's hope, had no thought for gain, the uncle had said. They were ready to run in the precisely opposite direction: to their *loss*.

These words left Angelin stunned. The uncle had gone on talking, longer than he ever talked before, until his nephew interrupted him to ask if there were not blood to be claimed by their family.

From one moment to the next, the uncle's speech slowed down, became as heavy and bare as the flagstones in a mausoleum. Yes, within their very own family, there was a blood that had not been taken back. That was the very reason that he had taken to the roads in midwinter. The Communists may have stolen their pastures and a part of their herd, but they couldn't take away the command of the blood. Yes, sure, they had tried to do that too. At school and in meetings they had said time and again that young people should be ready to lay down their lives for the ideas of Lenin, but everyone knew now that that business was finished. . . . Yes, so there was a blood to be reclaimed by their family, and neither he, nor his children, nor his children's children, would ever be able to escape it.

Angelin interrupted his uncle once again to ask for the name of the blood debtor. Then they both fell silent.

The day after the murder, remorse came faster than he had thought it would. The first night, he had waited in vain for sleep to come. On the second night too. What came to him instead was a vision of the blue necktie of his victim at the moment when he fell. It had waved to the side, as if wanting to stay up in the air a little longer, while its owner fell to the ground. Angelin had long dreamed of having such a fine tie, and he imagined he could see it coming toward his own neck. Since its owner was now not of this world, nothing stopped the tie from being his. . . .

He had told his sister all that in the course of the many hours they had spent together after the execution. He had waited a long time for an order to obey. No such thing came to him from any quarter, so he yielded to what cropped up on his path — the *Kanun*. As soon as he had carried out the act, he realized that the order was wrong. But it was too late. . . .

As she recounted the hours she and her brother had spent together since the fatal act, Mark could easily imagine the two of them in conversation. Oddly enough, he could only imagine it as a conversation between two naked bodies, both of them stripped and scrubbed, as if in preparation for leaving the world, beside a grave, or awaiting a postmortem. My God, he thought, that is exactly when they must have committed incest!

She finally got around to explaining the reason for their visit. Her explanations became more and more confused. Her brother was now entangled in the blood feud, because of the murder, and was therefore unable to do anything useful for anybody. For example, he couldn't go to Kosovo, where the insurrection had now broken out. He would either have to hide, or risk the revenge of the other clan, or give himself up to the authorities. In any case, nothing could now stop the blood from following its course. Whether he took refuge in the highlands or behind prison bars or in the grave, he had no means of stopping the wheels of the machine. If he went into hiding or into prison, then the opposing clan would kill someone else in his stead. If he were to die, then his own clan would be drawn into the infernal cycle. So everything would unfold along lines laid down centuries ago. And that was also the main cause of his distress: he had wanted to put a situation to right, to do something for others, and he found he had done precisely the opposite. As for knowing how to atone for his act, he . . . or rather, she and he (it had to be the two of them, Mark thought, with her white body laid out beside his thin and waxen shape, on the dissecting table) . . . well, they had had long arguments over it, because Angelin, against his sister's strong advice, had resolved to give up his life. However, the *Kanun* did not permit suicide, so he had thought of asking for help from the state . . . and that was why they had come to see Mark.

The painter was on the verge of saying, But why here, in my studio? when his eyes strayed toward his old traveling chest. That was where his other dress must be hidden — a police uniform . . . or a snakeskin!

You're such a dolt, Mark told himself. Obviously they had to come to see you. Aren't you the next deputy chief of police?

Coming face-to-face with death had led them to be the first to discover the great secret of his own life. They'd guessed what no one else had yet seen. For Angelin and his sister, from now on, the other world where Mark would have been the deputy chief of police was the only one that mattered.

Mark needed some time to measure fully what they were asking. The only way to block the mechanism that Angelin had set in motion — to halt the rusty gearwheels that even death could no longer arrest — was to have recourse to another machine, the machinery of state. The plan was simple: the young man would give himself up to the police, and the state would give him a heavy sentence, the harshest of all. Not fifteen years in jail, as the current law required, but capital punishment. At a time like the present when laws were changing from day to day and cases were batted back and forth between Tirana and the Council of Europe, that was a conceivable plan. So the boy would be judged and sentenced, then shot like most murderers. His only request was that in this case the state would assume the role of the opposing clan's executioner. He was perfectly aware that in ordinary circumstances such a request would be considered insane. But in current conditions, with so many Albanian issues going to Brussels and Strasbourg and suchlike, and also more especially because the National Ferment

Party was demanding that the ancient *Kanun* be incorporated in the revised penal code, everything was possible. So that . . .

Mark rubbed his forehead from time to time — the best way to restore the flow of blood to his brain when it was slowing down.

So, in that way, by inserting the state into the system, the circle of revenge would be automatically squared. The family — that's to say, us, she said, pointing to her breast — would claim its blood (she pointed to her brother) not from the Shkreli, but from the state!

The two of them then expanded on their plan and expressed themselves quite clearly. Shifting the claiming of the blood into a new, unprecedented area made it all different. The state was accustomed to facing enemies. It could tolerate and maintain hostilities more easily than any clan. It all hung on whether the state would consent to the plan; that is to say, whether it would agree to pronounce the brother's sentence not just as an expression of the law and the penal code, but also as an expression of the rules of the *Kanun*. Furthermore, the two of them insisted that in the death certificate that the prosecutor and the coroner would sign after the execution (or else in the report of it that would be published in the records), the following wording would have to be used: "The State of Albania has shot Angelin of the Ukaj, cleansing the blood of Marian Shkreli, its servant."

Mark took his head in his hands, as if to stop it bursting. He hadn't interrupted throughout his girlfriend's long explanation. When she finished, he asked what he thought was a whole variety of questions, but it all boiled down to a single query: "So you think the state should become a player in the feud?" And every time she answered "Yes, exactly," her eyes flashed with an icy gleam that seemed to say, And what's so strange about that? Throughout its long life the state has done nothing but kill and slaughter people. You yourself are in a better position than anyone to know that!

In other circumstances Mark would have shouted back, "Why me?" But it was too late now. He drew himself up to his full height, and though he said nothing, his whole body, like a dancer's, expressed a single thought: Of course I am.

Of course he was.

None of them had been watching the clock. It must have been near dawn when Mark promised to put in a word with the police chief or the prosecutor in the morning, or, if the opportunity arose, with the two of them.

Mark, Angelin, and his sister were all dead tired. The two visitors got up to take their leave. Mark went to the bay window, looked outside, and declared that they would perhaps be better advised to wait for dawn.

He showed them the bed where he only rarely spent the night and stretched out on the sofa. For a long while he thought he could hear snatches of their whispering to each other, which sounded to him like so many lovers' sighs.

As the first rays of light came through the window, he remembered she had taken the pill, which reassured him, and he fell asleep immediately.

When he woke, he knew intuitively that they had already left. He moved around the empty bed, thinking he could recognize her smell, which he knew so well, but then suddenly turned his eyes away, as if afraid of finding something revolting.

It looked like a fine day outside. The prosecutor was nowhere to be found. As for the police chief, Mark ran into him as he was leaving his office.

"I was sure we'd run into each other someday," the chief said warmly.

Mark was no longer surprised by anything. The idea that the chief had also foreseen and even expected this meeting seemed natural.

"Listen, do you want to come with me? I have to go out of town, and on the way we'll have all the time you need to tell me about your request."

Mark was tempted to answer that he had no request to make, but the chief didn't let him get a word in. As he got into the car, he confided that he had always enjoyed the company of artists. To back this up, he nodded toward a literary review lying on the rear seat. Then he leaned toward the driver, presumably to whisper directions in his ear.

"You won't be bored," he told Mark. "Quite the opposite. I think you'll have a great time."

Just my luck! Mark thought. I could do without that — watching someone get arrested! This whole business could have begun far more simply — like, with forms to fill out.

"Despite all the work I get loaded with, I do try to find the time to read," the police chief went on. "Of course, I don't really grasp all the contemporary stuff. You know, in that issue there, for instance, there are some poems. . . . How should I say . . . Well, I would really like your opinion, at least on one of them, the one that mentions the Grand Duchy of Luxembourg. . . ."

Mark leafed through the magazine until he found the poem. A moment later, he burst out laughing.

"You see!" the police chief exclaimed. "You're an artist, but even you couldn't help yourself laughing. That proves there's something not quite right."

"That's true enough," Mark said.

"Please read me the first two lines. I'd like to hear them said by you."

Mark began to recite the verse aloud:

> *I shall come unto you dressed in sackcloth*
> *Wearing Luxembourg as a condom*

They guffawed in unison for a while. Then the policeman expressed his fear that the lines might be seen as offensive to the duchy. "We mustn't forget that tiny Luxembourg is a member-state of the European Union!" Mark shrugged his shoulders. The chief went on: "What I say to myself is this: if you allow someone to refer to Luxembourg or Denmark as condoms, what would you say if someone else wanted to describe you — I mean, your country — as, let's say, a chamber pot? That would be shocking, wouldn't it? The land of eagles . . . a toilet bowl?"

Mark laughed again.

They had left the town and were driving toward the highlands. Mark could barely stop himself asking where they were heading. From time to time he told himself that the farther they got from town, the easier it would be to broach the subject he was anxious to discuss.

At last they came to a halt at the edge of a copse.

"Beautiful scenery, isn't it?" the police chief said. "I told you you wouldn't be bored."

He got out first, and looked around. The driver opened the trunk and took out a blanket and two bottles of water, which he set down beside his boss.

Mark and the policeman sat down as if they were about to have a picnic.

"Marvelous scenery, you must admit," the chief said again.

Then he took a pair of binoculars from his bag and began to adjust the focus.

"I have to look at something," he said suddenly as he put the binoculars to his eyes.

What a magnificent police force! No two ways about it! Mark thought, ironically. God alone knew what there could be to observe in these boondocks.

"Do you want a turn?" the other man asked as he offered Mark the binoculars.

Mark took the instrument, placed it on the bridge of his nose, and steered it toward the area that the police chief had been watching. As he turned the focus knob, the mountains raced nearer with frightening speed. He thought he could make out the overgrown bushes that masked what was supposed to be the secret entrance to the deep storage depot of the National Archives. A strange association of ideas brought his girlfriend's genitals to mind. Then he thought of the head of state making his way into the depot the day after assuming supreme power.

He was intensely eager to learn something more about that whole story. But he restrained himself, remembering he had vowed to ask no questions until he had managed to get the main matter off his chest.

He handed the binoculars back to their owner, and with a slight feeling of guilt repeated the police chief's own words back to him:

"What a marvelous view! . . ."

He sensed that he was being looked at sourly. Was the chief so naive as to think no ill? Maybe he ought to interrogate the policeman about some case or other. About the bank holdup, for instance. Or even, so as to seem even more loyal, to ask him if they had any chance, from their vantage point, of seeing the robbers on the move.

He made up his mind to ask that question and waited for the chief to put down the binoculars before speaking.

When his companion lowered his arm, Mark saw that his eyes had gone quite empty, as if their former liveliness had stayed stuck to the viewfinder. He must have seen something, Mark thought to himself. Something he would rather not have seen. How else could he account for the policeman's expression, halfway between weariness and annoyance?

"Unless I'm mistaken, you have something to say to me," the police chief said at last.

Mark took a deep breath before launching into his subject. The policeman listened without interrupting once. He batted his eyelids several times, then opened them wide before shutting them completely.

"Hmm, so that's what it's about," he mumbled when Mark had finished, then took up the binoculars again.

He looked into the far distance for a moment.

"So that's what it's all about," he repeated, as if he could see in the viewfinder whatever it was that had surprised him.

"I'm not asking for an immediate answer," said Mark. "I do realize that my request is extremely unusual. I must ask you once again to forgive me."

"Fine, fine," the policeman murmured.

Mark wanted to break the ice that had formed between them by moving on to some other topic, something harmless or amusing. He had only worried that the police chief would answer him with a decisive no.

As he racked his brains for a subject that might lighten the atmosphere, maybe something about the NYPD methods featured in the papers recently, or about the training some Albanian policemen were getting in America to learn about those methods, he stumbled onto a quite different tack and came out with the view that humanity, up to the present, had been following a completely wrong path.

The police chief began to listen with rapt attention. I must be crazy, Mark thought, to choose a time like this to start philosophizing!

"Could I look through the binoculars one more time?" he asked point-blank, perhaps to avert a complete rupture between the two of them.

The policeman handed him the glasses.

"If you should happen to see anything suspicious, let me know. Meanwhile, I'll have a little nap."

Mark stretched out his hand and took the binoculars. He had never imagined things would proceed in such an ordinary way.

He clapped the instrument to his eyes and directed it once more toward the mountainside. And as before, the mountains swooped first to the left, as if to shake off the snow from their peaks and shoulders, then to the right, and then came to a relative degree of rest. The summits stayed icy sharp, all the same, and the dark streaks etched into their sides seemed to have no intention of reaching an arrangement with the world down below. "If you happen to see anything suspicious, let me know," Mark mumbled, repeating the policeman's words like an incantation. As the chief was asleep, that meant that he, Mark, was now deputizing for him. You could tell he was asleep by the change in his breathing and by the regular dilation of his nostrils. Up above, in fact, everything looked suspicious, even the foreign body that had fallen from the sky — the snow.

Lord, what is the great sin that has been committed and is all around us? Mark wondered. He immediately realized why the whole world looked suspicious to him. It was because of the dense mass of brambles that hid the tunnel that led to the Secret Archives. As they resembled a woman's entrance, so they spread the awareness of sin far and wide. His mistress had cheated on him for sure during her stay in Tirana, and afterward too. Maybe even with her own brother. He steadied the binoculars with both his hands. As he was almost certain that the tunnel's entrance was on the narrow rocky shelf he had in his view, he was expecting to pierce its secret any minute now. On the surface of the human body, there were only two small spy-holes through which the image of the outside world could enter the inner darkness. The terrestrial globe must also have a similar passageway through which you could go from one zone to the other. Men had been looking for it for thousands of years, to no avail. He thought of Ulysses sacrificing a sheep, three thousand years ago, in the hope that the smell and color of its blood would help him find the passage.

Mark could hear the police chief snoring, as if in the far distance. He propped himself up on an elbow, to hold the binoculars more steadily.

Up in the heights, the undergrowth was rustling in an anxious wind. All around, everything seemed unsettled and expectant. Guilt might suddenly make its appearance; Mark was afraid of dozing off and missing it.

Don't drop off! he ordered himself. Keep the vigil a little longer. You only get one chance at this in a lifetime.

And then they did indeed begin to appear, in a long line. Not the bank robbers, but a procession of official cars. The first to stop was a long black limousine, but the man who stepped out of it was not the Albanian dictator. His beetle-like eyebrows gave him away: Mark recognized Leonid Brezhnev, the former leader of the Soviet Union. Next to step out was Walter Ulbricht, and behind him two cloaked figures costumed as for a fancy-dress ball.

They're all looking for the same thing, Mark thought.

He was sure that the Guide of the Albanian People, though he had been here once before, would return. He wouldn't miss his chance to be in this parade of rubble.

And indeed Hoxha did come, but he arrived late — which was a deception, of course, since he was actually early, doing everything as he always did, back to front, like the registration plate on his limousine. As tricky as ever! Mark exclaimed.

For a brief instant the lenses clouded over. Then a flurry, which could have been a cloud of dust or a shower of dried violet petals, signaled the arrival of another high personage. He came in a black carriage with wide-spoked wheels, and he climbed down with some difficulty. Well, well, Mark said to himself, here comes Oedipus Rex! . . . The old man stumbled forward as he turned the black holes of his eyes this way and that.

So there you are at last! Mark almost said aloud, but then he realized he was not in the least surprised. It seemed he had been expecting this arrival since the beginning of his vigil.

Unhappy monarch! he thought. You are the only one in this whole crowd of murderers to have truly repented. Yes, you alone, you strange hybrid of good and bad fortune!

He was strangled by emotion, and his hand shook. The picture in the viewfinder could hardly stay still and nearly collapsed for good.

Mark could see that the old king was still in pain as he continued to turn his empty sockets in all directions. Mark wanted to say something to him, to share with him things that were bursting out of his imagination, but he did not know what language to use. O man of mystery, son and father of yourself, why did you shoulder a crime that you did not commit?

Mark was convinced he had always known what suddenly became clear: that Oedipus had not killed his own father. Nor had he ever been his mother's lover. These legends were just symbols of possible offenses — declared to have already been committed the day that Oedipus became a tyrant.

Mark's mind was as incandescent as burning coal. Every tyrant is a potentially infinite sequence of crimes. On the very day that a tyrant seizes the crown, those crimes are transferred from the future, from what is yet to come, to the past, to its furthest reaches, as far as that surest haven of rest, the mother's womb. . . .

Through the misty lens of the binoculars, on the other side of the valley, Mark could see Oedipus still rolling his absent eyes. O blind tyrant! Mark shouted out once again, O father and son of sin, what are you seeking with your non-eyes?

But the old man kept on poking the undergrowth with his walking stick, seeking the mysterious door to the tunnel from which he had once, by mistake, emerged, hoping to delve back down into the dark. . . .

A week later, Mark Gurabardhi received an answer from the legal and police authorities. The state declined to amend its regulations to conform to the rules of the *Kanun*. Among the reasons given for this refusal was a recent circular from the Council of Europe that seemed to have some indirect bearing on the matter.

Mark read the letter several times over. He stopped for a long while on the word *Europe,* staring at it so hard that it seemed to wobble, then to go hazy, as if trying to erase itself forever.

He raised his eyes to the sky as if in response to a call from on high. But the sky was tiresomely void. He was aware that a vacuum can have immense destructive force, but this was the first time he had come up against such a feeling of oppression. The clouds stood stock-still, and the birds, who seemed to be in collusion, had all flown away. Things must have looked more or less like that at the start or the end of the season when, as people have always supposed, the gods deserted Earth. A sky bereft of its masters, a sky in mourning stretching to infinity. Who knows why the gods left? Where in the universe did they go?

Mark didn't know why, but he felt like crying.

Tirana–Paris, 1998–2000